The Last Call

By

J.E. Hollins

Prologue

Ok guys, let's double time it!! We're going to be late. Ron check on your little brother. Melanie are you dressed?

"Yes, mom. I've been dressed for twelve min... (looks at the clock on her phone) and twenty-four, twenty-five Twenty-six seconds", Melanie finished sarcastically while rolling her eyes. She only did that because she was in her room and not in her mom's vision. She knew better.

"I can hear the eye-rolling in your voice. Don't make me come up there!" Because Melanie was the only girl, she had the privilege of having the other room on the second floor. Down the hall from their mom.

"Sorry. I'm ready". Melanie quickly adjusted her attitude. She rarely gives her mom trouble. She was just sick of church. But she knew better to voice her opinion. She remembered what happened when Ron felt like he had a say in the matter a year back.

"Well, if you're ready, head towards the door, please."

"Yes, mam"

Ron, Ken, you guys at the door?

"Yes, mam". The two young men answered. "But Ken is carrying that dang dog in his hands. He's trying to bring him to church with us. I told him to put him down but he ain't listening.

"We can't leave him, mom. He's not a dog, he's a puppy. He's just a baby, mom. Can he come? He'll die if we leave him here alone...little Ken ended up pouting. Being the youngest of the bunch at the age of seven, he felt rather protective of the small animal. He was finally the "big brother" and took responsibility very seriously.

Ken, please put Snoop back in his kennel. He won't die from the few hours we'll be gone. We'll stop and get him a treat on our way back home, okay?

Ken answered reluctantly, hanging his head down sadly as he walked back down the hall to his room where Snoop's kennel was kept. He returned to the front room with slumped shoulders as he looked daggers at his big brother for snitching.

He was going to ask his mom once she saw how much of a big boy he was. Getting dressed in record time and all. And without any prodding from his mom this Sunday morning.

Mom turned the corner in a frenzy, mentally checking off her list.

Keys, purse, Bible… SH!#! She mumbled the expletive as she remembered her Sunday School book left upstairs on her nightstand. She silently asked God for forgiveness for losing control of her language and hurried upstairs to retrieve her book.

As she chided herself for not telling Melanie to grab this week's lesson, the phone rang.

Brring… Bbbrring… Bbrrriiinngg!!

She figured she'd pick it up as she entered her room.

"Just a minute!" she shouted as if the inanimate object could hear or answer back.

"Why does it seem that that d@×m phone gets louder the longer it takes to answer it?"

She snatched the receiver out of her purse and yelled into it, clearly irritated.

"What!!"

"Angelica Watson?" came the male voice on the other end.

"Who's asking?" Angel (Angelica's nickname) was not in the mood for any nonsense, especially since she didn't recognize the voice.

"Is this Angelica Watson?" The voice asked again, patiently and peacefully, knowing the answer.

Angelica sighed aggressively, really not wanting to be late for church.

"WHO IS THIS?!" she asked loudly, this time preparing to hang up.

The person on the other end paused, then answered.

"This is… God."

Table of Contents

CHAPTER 1: The Mask

Angel paused, her patience pushed to the limit. *"Excuse me?"* she said, completely unimpressed and ready to *pop off* any second.

"I just wanted to inform you that I'm on my way," replied the caller.

Angelica sighed, facing the difficult decision of whether to completely lose her religion at that moment or keep it… *she lost it. "WHAT THE HELL KIND OF JOKE IS THIS? YOU GOT ME CONF…"*

"No confusion, my child. You only have a short amount of time before my return, and due to your representation of me of late and because of my love for you, I wanted to give you a chance to make things right."

All she heard was the word *love*, and she realized who it must have been on the other line.

"WESS!? Really!? Man, I'm going to be late for my Sunday school class, fooling' with you. This is not funny, and you're not cute!" She was just about to slam the phone back on the receiver when the voice called her by her childhood name. *Ally*. One, she knew that only family and *close* friends called her. And come to think of it, how did Wess know? He had only known her for just a few weeks before their mutual decision to end their short... association.

"Angel, you still love Sunday school. To the point that you've been a teacher of it as early as your teen years. Seventeen, I understand. I loved the love you had of sharing my word. You seem to keep the knowledge to share with others, but clearly, you've forgotten to keep it in your heart."

"I know the death of your parents hurt you. To the point of causing your faith to waver. I know, and I understand. But now, I will always love you. I know you know this because this is the lesson you planned to teach this morning. But please remember what I commanded. You must be Holy, for I am Holy. Remember, I am just. Forgiving. Remember my love for you."

Something changed in the atmosphere during the conversation with the person on the phone. She began to feel in her heart that the call wasn't a joke.

Not only did the caller know about her young life, but her plans for today seemed *accurate!* And the feeling she felt was indescribable: peace, no fear, no hatred.

She didn't feel... *rushed.* Time was no more.

Once she gave the caller her full attention, she couldn't speak. All she could do was weep. Then she began to pour out her heart...

"My God, My God! Please, please, please."

She couldn't finish her thoughts; she tried between sobs... *"I know I have been angry. I know I haven't trusted you like I said I would. My relationships haven't been pleasing. My language. How I communicate with my children. I know you have given me time. I know you've given me grace..."*

"Remember my love for you. I'll always love you."

The voice said with finality in their voice. Angelica rushed in...

"I know, I know and I promi.." CLICK...

Suddenly came the sound from the other end...

It was then that Angelica realized she hadn't opened her mouth. Well, she *knew* she was speaking, communicating, something...! She was pouring out her heart. She *knew* it! But she had still been crying, too. Completely unable to utter even *one* word. But she felt in her heart that whoever she was speaking... well, communicating with, knew and understood her *every* word.

Or was it her thoughts?

She looked and also realized that she was on her knees...

She quickly scrambled onto her feet. Forgetting her Sunday school book.

The reason is she even came upstairs in the first place.

She quickly rushed down the stairs, almost falling as she slipped on the last two.

"Mom, you ok?"

Ron hurriedly rushed in when he thought she'd fallen down the stairs. She sounded *so* anxious. He knew she always wore high heels to church and felt that she may have lost her footing in her haste to get to church on time.

But before she could even answer, he witnessed the look on her face.

Her countenance... she… seemed... *different.*

What on earth?! He thought.

"......Mom...you, ok? What's going on? Were you running down the stairs? DID YOU FALL??!! She'd been upstairs for only a couple of minutes. Why was she rushing? They still had plenty of time to get to church. He remembered the phone rang and she called out her intention to answer it AND to get her book for Sunday school.

"Who was on the phone? What did they say?"

Before he could voice more questions, his mom began to cry. I mean, cry! Come to think of it, she seemed like she'd been crying already. Her cry was like soft but gut-wrenching sobs, and she stretched out both of her arms to pull him in for a hug. It was really more of an embrace. And the moment they connected, he was inexplicably compelled to embrace her back. And he simply began to weep. His two other siblings rounded the corner and came to a halt.

The two had a moment of confusion. Angel and Ron turned around and opened their arms to welcome the two into the embrace without even uttering one word. And just like that, Angel's only daughter and her youngest child joined them. And the family sobbed for what seemed to the unit an eternity. Although nothing was said or even explained, there appeared to be an unspoken agreement. Whatever was happening, it seemed to be what the family needed. Even though the moment was entirely outside of their own conscious understanding.

Eventually, once again in silent agreement, the group slowly relaxed their embrace. Ron was the first one to speak. Clearly, no one else could find the words to express what the family had just experienced...WAS experiencing.

"So...mom...?" He offered. Knowing that spoke for everyone.

"Baby, I know," says Angelica. *I don't have any answers to your questions, but I know who does."* She grabs Ron by the hand. He grabs Melanie's hand, and Melanie grabs Ken's hand. Seeing the confused, even scared look in his eyes, she gives it a slight

squeeze to assure him that everything is going to be better from this day forward. For some strange reason, she knows her thoughts to be true.

The family bowed their heads as the matriarch led them in prayer.

As the prayer came to an end and the family began to lift their heads, Angelina's cell phone rang......

CHAPTER 2: Healed

"Alright, baby," Darrell smoothly whispered in his phone. He was waiting in the chair at the barber's for his turn. He had to keep his waves tight. He knew he was known for that. That was part of his swag. He loved how all eyes were on him when he entered a building or walked into a room. And as far as the ladies were concerned... well, let's just say there was absolutely no problem. "Baby, I'm just craving your body," he continued. In what, he disillusioned himself into thinking, was said low enough for only the lovely lady on the other end to hear. But the next statement heard from Benny, his barber, proved him wrong. "Alright, Darrell, you and wifey are going to have to get a room. You're up, and my ears are too pure to be privileged to that kind of talk."

"I ain't interested," Benny, the owner of the shop and the very one who has kept Darrell's hair right since he was a pre-teen, snapped at Darrell as he fired up his clippers.

"Come on, Deacon. Shut it down. At least until you're out of my chair. But don't forget to give Donna my love first," referring to Darrell's beautiful wife. He reluctantly heard all the sweet and sexy sayings of the conversation. A conversation that needed to be held in the bedroom. He couldn't help but shake his head. He had known the young man since Darrell's childhood. Around the age of ten years or so. He remembered when he came to live with his grandparents. He knew there was a story around that but never felt it was his place to ask questions about what a private family thing was. Benny even cut the young minister's hair for the two most important days of his life: his wedding and the day he was appointed and ordained as Deacon in the ministry of Heavenly Highway Baptist.

He remembered when Darrell came to him for a fresh cut for his first date with the young lady that eventually became Darrell's wife. He laughed to himself when he reminisced on how Darrell had to wait until his head dried because of the film of sweat that formed on the crown of the young one's head due to nerves of going on a date with Chanel... the most beautiful girl in Northland High.

"OFF! YOUNG MAN!" Benny firmly, albeit playfully commanded. Secretly happy to see that the couple still lived that "Newlywed" life. If he stood corrected, it's been at least ten or eleven years since the wedding.

"Hey baby, gotta go. Benny is threatening to shave my head bald if I don't get off. I'll see you later tonight. That alright?

Before Darrell could completely severe the connections a drop-dead creature, even with the engorged state of her mid-section due to the twins she was carrying, walked thru the door.

"You guys are something else," Benny said, shook his head, and laughed. You guys can't get enough of each other."

Calvin snapped his head up as his wife walked, or waddled, through the shop's entrance. No one noticed his slight wide-eyed look or nervous chuckle.

"What are you babbling about Benny?" Darrell's wife, Chanel, feigned indignance as she reached up while cradling her stomach, to plant a quick daughterly kiss on the older man's cheek.

"Don't listen to this old geezer baby, he's just hating on our love. Wachu doing here?" Benny halted, cutting Darrell's hair. Giving the young couple time to greet one another properly.

Darrell gave his wife, Chanel, a proper husbandly kiss and hug. Also giving her mid-section a father-to-be hug and kiss.

"I can't believe that's the truth. Benny, how long have you and Delores been married again?" Chanel asked, feeling absolutely certain that Benny had no reason to feel any type of hatred regarding anyone's relationship. Being married longer than either one of them had been alive.

"Young lady, I don't even think I can even count that high," he laughed. He started to finish the job on the young man's head when he felt moisture forming and gave Darrell a stern look.

"What's up with your young man? Your wife got you so hot and bothered that you are sweating'!?" He scolded playfully.

Darrell laughed nervously again. Then recovered quickly before anyone could catch on.

"Well you know how it is Benny. Look at my baby. Can you blame me?" Darrell answered, thinking quickly.

"Aww, thank you, sweetie," Chanel gushed as she bent over to plant a sweet and loving kiss on her husband's lips.

He slightly brushed her display of affection off with the excuse of needing to go to the bathroom.

"Thanks baby". Darrell unfolded his six-foot five-inch frame of the barber's chair.

"Let me stick my head under the hand dryer in the bathroom and dry off this effect you have on me woman!!" He gave her a quick peck as he hurriedly approached the men's room. He walked straight into the bathroom and headed to grab a few paper towels to wipe away what he knew was more guilt than his libido that was causing the perspiration to suddenly appear on his head. He deleted the evidence of his last caller. As he started to wave his hands to activate the electronic paper towel release, his phone rang. "Man! He thought to himself, what if the phone had rung just a minute earlier! He'd have been sweating bullets!!

He looked at the caller ID on his iPhone, but no number was displayed. Curiously, he answered.

"Hello". Came out wondering who this could be.

"Hello, my dear son," came a voice that was unfamiliar. The endearment "dear son" threw him off.

"Who's this?" Darrell was really confused. No one had ever called him son in his thirty-eight years of life, not even his grandfather, who had raised him and was the closest thing he had as a dad, other than Benny the barber.

"I just wanted to tell you about my coming, my child", came the unfamiliar voice again.

There goes that reference to being his child again. Both his Grandparents have passed, and they'd be the only ones qualified to call him son. Not that they ever did. And he hadn't spoken to either of his biological parents, if you can call them that, over the last three decades.

"Once again, who is this!" Darrel just wanted to hear the voice again to see if there was any recollection.

"My child, you wouldn't recognize my voice even if I continued to speak to you. You seemed to have decided to ignore my voice for a while now. It seems you no longer can recognize my voice even though I never stopped speaking to you. Whether listening or not, my beloved. I needed to let you understand I'm returning."

Darrell squinted his eyes, trying to concentrate on the voice on the other end. There was something so familiar but distant about it. He couldn't say what he wanted to say. ...his heart raced as a feeling of sorrow.... guilt? Repentance...something life-altering came over him...

"Who is this?" Darrell asked...fearing but needing to know the answer... Who is...

"You recognize my voice now, my child?" I know it's hard to let go of the past on your own. Understand that there is no one on Earth who understands true love. You received my love once. But you've somehow lost your way. I've never left you. I will never leave nor forsake you...

".... who is this?" Darrell asked ever so softly in a moment of surrender. Almost so childlike that he didn't recognize HIS own voice.

"I'm God," came the caller's reply.

"... so, God has a cell phone?" Darrell chuckled nervously. Trying to shake off the feeling that washed over him the minute he answered his phone. What on Earth was this about?

The conversation quickly reverberated thru his mind. The word my son used more than once.... is this his father! A mixture of feelings ran thru him. The thought that no good jerk, the one who was supposed to be called "his dad," would have the nerve to contact him, playing games, made him pass furious!!

"Dad?!" He yelled into the device

"No, my son. I'm the Father.

"Father!? I figured it was you. You Lousy piece of.."

"My child, this is THE FATHER."

Something about the caller caught Darrell's attention. It MADE him pay attention.

"I don't know who this is but I don't find this funny," Darrell said with his bite, albeit still irritated. He looked at his phone again to see if the caller's number was displayed on his caller ID. But no such luck. It said, "Unknown caller". Getting back to the stranger on the other end, he continued, "I don't know who you're used to dealing with, but you got the wrong one, buddy!" Darrell prepared to end the call when the caller at the end of the line says, in a calmness that Darrell couldn't name, but it changed his whole attitude. And a piece that was so inexplicable he had to put into it. And not reluctantly, he admitted to himself. He admitted to surrendering to.... whatever was happening…

"I just wanted you to know that I've never left your side. My love for you is eternal. A coming back for my children" was the caller's final statement.

Then Darrell heard what sounded like a click from the other end of the line."

Darrell stood for several minutes, pondering what had just happened. He leaned on the sink in total confusion but in complete peace, all at once. He turned around and looked at himself in the mirror. For some strange reason, he looked...different. Observing the moisture rolling down his face, he pondered, how long had he been crying?

Chapter 3: Grace

The music was deafening as Tripp (aka Trever) bobbed his head to the beat while waiting for his "associate," who he knew better, to have good news! He spotted the top of a familiar head.

He saw his boy Zipp, making his way through the crowd of clubbers. Zipp was named for how quickly he gets things done. If you wanted something or someone handled quickly or discretely, he was your guy.

As Zipp, whose real name was William, made it halfway towards Tripp, he stopped to grab a sexy young woman , who was twerking on some clown and planted a kiss on the female. Who, to the indignation of her partner, didn't seem to mind one bit. And the dude with her knew not to even flinch. Zipp's reputation proceeded him. He palmed the receiving young lady's behind before smoothly moving and bopping his way toward Tripp. Tripp and Zipp sounded corny. Like some kind of comedy act. But that would be your first and last mistake if they ever got wind that you tried to clown on them.

As Zipp finally made it to him, he shook hands and dapped it up. Tripp nodded his head towards the corner VIP section area. An arrangement he had with the owner for whenever he or any of his crew had business to conduct. Or just some much needed chill time. That spot was reserved for them, and after they greeted they made their way to their area. Tripp gave a quick wave to the attending server who knew their usual.

'So what's sup Tripp gave Zipp an all knowing glare. Wanting to know if some certain "business" was handled.

It's all good, bro. Zipp returned an all knowing look. Reassuring him that he lived up to his reputation. Quick and discreet. That's how he does it!

Good, let's celebrate. Tripp nodded as the server came right on cue with their usual order of steak and bottles of Dom Pe'rignon champaign. The server removed himself quietly, giving the gentlemen—the term is used loosely—their usual privacy.

"*So wudup*", Zipp asked Tripp. He just finished his job, but he wasn't going to relax until Tripp gave the word.

"Man, we good. Just chill. We goo...", Tripp's statement was interrupted by the ringing of his cell. The one that he only conducted business with.

"Yea!" snapped Tripp. He was looking forward to some downtime for himself. Whoever, this was better have some big numbers on their minds.

"My beloved...my Son, I just wanted to tell you that I'm on my way. And because of my love for you, I wanted to give you a chance to get right before my return".

Tripp waited for the punchline. Nothing came.

"Who the hell is this?! He was immediately irritated.

He answered the phone only because it was his business line. Only a few privileged clientele had access. And even though he wasn't feeling "work," he knew that business was business. So he answered the call. But this was some bull.

"Who is this." he snapped again, gaining his guy's attention.

"S'up!! "Zipp leaned forward, one hand on his weapon, the other he grabbed Tripp's arm. He was already in defense mode for whatever was jumping off!

Tripp put up a finger to calm Zipp down. He was sure it was some kind of bad joke, which he knew had to be an even badder decision for the caller when he got done with them. Or maybe it's just a wrong number. He erased that thought. No one can get thru this line without his permission unless they are God. The caller responded calmly, seemingly unmoved by Tripp's clearly threatening tone.

"My child, I know it's been a while since we've spoken. But I wanted to remind you that I will always love you and have never forsaken you. I understand the decisions you've made in the last few years. I've covered and kept you because of my love for you. You are my child always, and it is never too late to come back home."

And at the beginning of the conversation Tripp was "ready to shut the whole situation down....but there was something about the caller's voice, the conversation... he couldn't quite call it but he knows he was no longer irate. As a matter of fact, the peace that he was currently experiencing...a peace that seemed to reach his mind, body AND spirit.... a peace that was inexplicable, just soothed his soul. And he changed his tone with the caller.

"Look, I don't know who you meant to call but you got the wrong.."
BRANDON, my son, my beloved son, it is you. I'm
calling. It's been a while since we've spoken. You probably can't recall my voice. It has been a while. I've never left your side. I have always been here. I've kept you and protected you from hurt, harm, and danger. You are never too loss for my love to not find you. Every situation, every bullet dodged, I was there protecting you. See, my son, you have a calling in your life. I have a plan for you. You, my son, have a purpose.

Tripp was stunted at the mention of his name. Who is this? It has been a minute since anyone called him Brandon. Who knew about the name that he hadn't heard since he'd been a little boy. Who knew about his life. The shoot outs,.. he had barely survived those moments in his life. He still had a bullet lodged in his pelvis, which caused a slight limp and sometimes caused pain from time to time. He usually just self-medicates - and when he says medicate, he meant drugs or alcohol, or both- but then, as usual, he kept on pushing.

"You know there is a better way to ease your pain, Brandon. I'm still here, knocking at the door." The caller interrupted Tripp's thoughts. Tripp's eyes automatically went to the club entrance, followed by Zipp's confused gaze, hand still on his peace. He jumped up. Tripp waved him back into his seat. Now, he really was confused, even a little panicky.

It's not in his nature to feel fear or anything close to that emotion. If anything, it was usually he and Tripp who caused fear. But he was feeling something unfamiliar.

Seeing something on Tripp's face made Zipp straighten up in his chair. He jester to Tripp to tell him what was going on. Who was on the line!

Tripp held up his hand again to calm him down. He knew something changed in the atmosphere and he couldn't yet explain it.

He kept his hand up as he rose from his chair and made his way past all the servers, clubbers, and bouncers and through the front door. He walked past the long line of folks waiting to get in the popular weekend spot. Some are clearly already filled with "party enhancements." He kept on past all of the luxury and sports vehicles, waiting for the valets to park them. Once he was halfway down the block, he knew he could ask the caller all the questions pleaguing him without interruption. The caller reiterated Tripp's thoughts. Yes, my son, now you can ask the questions you want to ask. It's just you and me. But suddenly, Tripp was almost tentative to do so.... Almost... he rushed his reply into the receiving end of his iPhone 13.

"Who are you?" Came Tripp's urgent question.

"Of course, you don't recognize my voice"! It's been some time since you and I have spoken... Past was annoyed at the caller because those words had already been said earlier. Tripp growled..

"WHO IS THIS??" Tripp repeated, throwing gritted teeth.

"My beloved… "I'm God"

Chapter 4: Family First

Angel wiped her eyes before addressing her children, who were struggling with their own need to understand what was happening. They shared a moment that was...inexplicable. They eyed the family's matriarch with both query and confusion. And admittingly fear.. Before she could offer a word to her children, her cell phone rang. She stiffened both tentatively and in anticipation. She took a big breath, eying her oldest child. Noticing his observant albeit very concerned gaze regarding his mom. He noted she seemed a bit frazzled. That really concerned him. He's never seen her be nothing but in complete control of ...a pillar of strength, no matter what situation their family may be facing.

Angel gripped her phone and clicked the button to answer. She paused for a second to brace herself, then answered, *"Hello?"*

"Sister Angelica?" came the familiar voice of the Superintendent of Sunday School at her family church. Angel relaxed her shoulders visibly in relief.

"Brother Douglas!" She let out a breath with mixed emotions. She didn't know if she was happy or disappointed that it wasn't the previous caller. After a second, she decided she was relieved. She was not sure she was prepared to continue the conversation she was having with the previous caller.

"What a surprise. Uhh, what can I do for you? The kids and I are just heading out. We should be their for Sunday School right, uhh on time..."

"I am so glad I caught you, then," Brother Douglas rushed in, sounding perplexed. But before sharing his reason his call something about her voice gave him pause so he interjected, "You OK? You seem a bit winded. Are the kids alright?" He asked in sincere concern. Charles Douglas, aka Superintendent Douglas, aka Deacon Douglas, was one of the kindest men of Angel's church, Gilliad Worship Center. He and his wife had been members since the doors opened. She passed away about five years ago. So, Deacon Douglas practically lives at the church. Everyone knew he loved his ministry, but they also knew his other reason for being at the church when the doors

opened and closed. Everyone also knew how astute he was so it didn't surprise Angel when he asked her 'was there anything wrong'..

"I'm good, we're good, actually. It's just been...uh, umm, you called? How can I help you Deac?"

Angel was still stuck in her disappointment about who was on the line while simultaneously feeling relieved about who was on the line. She was torn between shouting to the Deacon and to anyone and everyone about how she was feeling. She knew she probably should be confused, but she was still walking in the peace she had been feeling since her conversation this morning…

"I'm glad you and the children are well. I apologize if I've interrupted your morning routine, but I'm in a bit of a pickle, and I need your help."

"Sure... what can I do to help. Just name it.

Deacon Douglas let out a relieved sigh.

"Thank you so much, Sis Angel. I know you and Bro. Warren split up the youth Sunday School classes, but he had a family emergency this morning and won't be able to make it. And I know it may be a bit of a task, but I'm going to need to combine both classes this morning. You think you can also take the young men's class for me...just for this morning?

At his request, a light bulb clicked on in her head. It had only been a little over an hour since her morning spiritual experience, so she was feeling empowered like nothing before! She had to spread this feeling. She needed to tell everyone, and the church's youth seemed to be the idea group to start with!

"I'd be delighted, Deac. I have the perfect subject. You don't mind if I get off the scheduled lesson, do you? I promise you it'll still be relevant. You won't be disappointed!" The excitement in her voice was so infectious that Deacon Douglas felt compelled to answer in the same spirit.

"Cool! Just fantastic, Sis Angel! Well, I won't hold you and your family up one more second, then. I'll see you when you get here. Oh, and you'll be in the fellowship hall. There wasn't any room large enough to hold the class. I hope that's OK. He ended up a bit dubious, mentally crossing his fingers even though she couldn't see him.

That's actually perfect. The P.A. system is working, right?

"It sure is."

"Well cue it up, I have a serious question I need to ask my class this morning Deac, A very serious question!"

They both ended the call feeling satisfied and exited. One didn't have a clue why, while the other knew exactly what the Doctor ordered... and did mean THE Doctor!!!

"She eyed her family, observing they still had that wonderous look on their faces. She gave her oldest a comforting squeeze on the shoulder as she ushered them all out the door and to their car. Yes, today's lesson will be the most important one of their life!

"You guys jump in the car. I'm going to grab my Bible real quick and lock up. Ron, could you please make sure everyone puts their seat belts on for me? "

It sounded like a request, but he knew it was an order. He nodded his understanding, even though his head was reeling with a million questions about what he and his family had experienced. Why was she acting so normal? She was just going to church like something, and he didn't know what it was, but something just happened. Looking at his siblings, he could tell they were all thinking the same thing.

"Why ain't nobody..." Lil Ron started to say but was quickly hushed by Melanie as they all witnessed their mother heading towards the car.

"But..." she silenced him by pinching him on the arm. *"Ooww"* He yelled out, but he quickly got the message.

"What's going on?" Angel suspiciously asked the innocent faces as she handed Ron her purse and bible to guard, and she drove them to church. *"Nothing!"* Sang the three unanimously. The innocent looks on their faces made her chuckle. Only because she knew what their "Nothing" really meant. No matter. She had bigger fish to fry. She carefully backed her vehicle out of their driveway and then made her way to the church with purpose.

Whatever their issue would have to wait.

Chapter 5: Unexpected Turns

"Young man? Did you fall in?" Darrell was reminded of where he was at the sound of Benny's gravelly voice.

It was a second or two before he could even answer. He didn't want to leave this place. He wasn't talking about the men's bathroom. He didn't want to end his conversation with...

"Darrel?" Came the concerned voice of his wife next.

"Baby, are you OK?

"I'm good," he said as he rushed out of the men's room, clumsily Tripping over a patch of frayed rug from a year of clients, not wanting to alarm them.

"I was just.... um on my way out"

He was so busy looking down at the spot where he Tripp, feigning concern, he missed the look that passed between the other two. Without seeing their exchange he, in his mind, knew that there was definitely a look and probably a couple of questions about what took him so long.

Darrel didn't look at either one of them in the eye as he just quietly sat back in the barber's chair. He was very relieved when no questions were asked. He sat patiently as Benny finished with his haircut. He offered no explanation for his sudden, somber attitude.

As he rose from the chair, when the cut was finished, Chanel finally broke the silence...

"Sweetie, do you have a stomachache? Would you feel more comfortable going home so you can have some privacy...?"

Darrel looked back and forth among the only two at the shop and realized that what they were both thinking about was clearly his reason for taking an extended visit to the men's room.

"What"?... Nah, I'm good... He was going to try to offer a feeble explanation when both of his loved ones broke out in laughter.

And just like that, the atmosphere of peace was evident. He didn't want to or could not explain what happened to him in the men's room or how he was feeling. But he welcomed the love that was in the room, and he joined them in what was clearly a funny moment.

"OK, y'all got jokes, haha." Benny and Chanel were so busy laughing to notice the shift in the atmosphere. Or maybe the shift was just in him, Darrel thought. He looked at his beautiful wife and his heart was broken. She'd been amazing to him since the first day they met. He couldn't believe THEEE Chanel!! The most beautiful girl in the whole neighborhood even gave him a minute of her time!! She has been the sweetest presence in her entire existence. She is so amazing. Talented. Brilliant. Hilarious!! just everything any man could dream of! She actually said yes when he proposed.

He just couldn't believe his love... She really does love him. He couldn't believe his ears when she said yes to his marriage proposal. At first, he just wanted to make sure that he locked her in before she came to her senses and changed her mind. And here they are... in love...married... AND EXPECTING A CHILD!! His guilt felt heavier the more he realized how blessed he was. What had he been thinking?! He has a fantastic life with an amazing woman and what!?, he was just going to throw it all away for...what? who?

"Hey, baby"? Chanel's sultry voice interrupted his revelry, snapping her finger, trying to bring him back from wherever he had gone.

"Hey, are you OK? You know we can head home if you're not feeling well?" She waddled over to Darrell wrapping her arms around his waist displaying serious concern now.

HUH? What? Oh nah, baby. I'm good. Just drifting off. Actually, I was mentally organizing my day. I know we got your Dr's appointment. And I have a couple things I have to take care of, you know stop by the church, blah, blah. Just getting my mind right" Darrell assured his wife. Still shaking but hoping he masked his real, mental state of mind.

"OK, OK. Well, we better get going because little Junior needs nourishment before we do anything!!"

She turned to Benny. *"You done, Benny? "she* said, giving her protruding belly a telltale rub.

"Yea, you love birds. Head on out and get my grandchild something to eat!" Benny said, referring to their unborn child. Even though there wasn't actual DNA that connected him to the young couple, he knew their bond couldn't be any closer if they were related by blood.

Darrell extended his right hand and clasped the older gentleman's in a firm handshake, firmer than usual. Benny pulled the young man close embracing him briefly, feeling there was something else going on with Darrel and knew at the right time he'll share it with him. He kissed Chanell affectionately on her cheek. And waved them both as they both made their way to Darrell's SUV. He smiled as he witnessed

Darrell lovingly help his young bride safely into the vehicle, then scurry and fold his tall frame in the driver's seat.

Something in his heart told him to put the young couple on his prayer list. He knew how important they both were in the ministry, and that undoubtedly put a bullseye on their marriage. He knew this all too well. He picked up the broom and started to sweep away the clippings of hair that lay on the shop's floor. As he swept, he prayed, covering the couple. He knew that was the only answer to whatever was going on in their lives.

CHAPTER 6: Shadows of the Past

Tripp just stood at the end of the block. Everything in him wanted to slam his cell phone on the concrete ground. Not considering that all of his important contacts and information regarding his business was attached to the smart device. None of that crossed his mind. To him, the phone suddenly felt as if it was on fire, and he just wanted to get rid of the offending device. But in his spirit, he also felt as though he'd rather allow the device to burn his flesh than relinquish his grasp.

"Tripp!?" Came the voice of Zipp as he spotted Tripp down the street. He had frantically done a quick visual perusal of the area at the entrance of the club. He had no idea which direction his boy had gone so he just yelled out his name. He spotted

Tripp was just up the block a few yards, so Zipp jogged in his direction.

"Tripp!" He yelled again a bit louder, feeling completely confused. He couldn't believe his bro would just be caught standing out all in the open without any backup or protection or at least had Zipp with him. *What the hell is really going on?* He finally reached Tripp to see his best friend looking as if he was lost or hadn't heard his name being called. THEN, as he got closer, he really became alarmed. From the short distance, it seemed as if his boy's face was covered in blood…. *WHAT THE… tears?* He realized as he even got closer. He couldn't believe his eyes. He blinked a couple of times to clear his vision. *What's really going on? Tears.?... TRIPPP WAS ... CRYIN...?* He couldn't even finish the thought. Zipp approaches Tripp carefully.

"Hey bruh? What's going on?"

Tripp then dropped his cell phone as if startled at the sound of Zipp's voice. Zipp immediately retrieved the device, not even concerned about its condition. All of his attention was on his boy, who he noticed still hadn't said a word. He hadn't made any other move or gasp except dropping his phone.

"Yo, bruh, what's up?" Zipp said as he retrieved Tripp's iPhone 13, examining it to assess any permanent damage.

"Hey!" He said a bit louder as he grabbed Tripp's shoulder in an attempt to shake him out of whatever daze or "Tripp" he

was in. He didn't see his boy take anything when they were in the club together. But he was probably already blazed when he made it to the club. That also explained what was going on.

Tripp clearly got a hold of some bad, or ...perhaps some good, good shi...

Tripp started to walk when he heard his phone ringing in Zipp's hand and quickly looked at his friend of over twenty years, with a combination of fear and confusion.

"Who is it!?"

Zipp gave the cell a quick look and with a dismissive expression on his face replied, "It says *"Unknown"*.

He was just about to decline the call when Trippp yelled, *"No!"*

Zipp was startled at his boy's response but handed the offending piece of equipment to Tripp's outstretched hand.

"Just give me the phone."

"No problem, man. Here"

Zipp slipped Tripp with the iPhone, then stepped back, keeping his eyes closely on his friend as well as a firm grasp on his "piece" hidden in his waste underneath his jacket.

Tripp answered, still feeling a combination of fear and annoyance, his overall feeling is curiosity. Why would anybody feel that this was even remotely funny? Surely, they have to know that they immediately have put their lives in danger. He'd simply get his tech guys to trace the whereabouts of the idiot on the other end of the line. And once he got that info their life was done!! Tripp would make sure of that!

Tripp put the phone to his ear, *"Who is this I'm going to give you one last chance to tell me because I don't think this is even close to funny, not to mention you're wasting my time."*

Tripp tried his best to sound threatening, but he knew by the look on Zipp's face that he was failing. Something about the atmosphere had some kind of hold. He couldn't put his hand on it. It was too calm. He didn't feel threatened, and in his spirit, he didn't think this was a prank call. What he was feeling was peace, something that had eluded his life for some time.

"My son. I'm reminding you of my love for you. I've never left your side, and know that I'm coming back.

Know that my plans for you are for you to prosper and I am coming to receive my children. And we will return to the place which I have prepared. A blessed place for all. Know that no matter what you have done, my love has covered it all. Just turn back to me, my son. I'm waiting with open arms. My beloved, the time is now.... *"click"!*

Before Tripp could offer any response, the line was severed. Tripp didn't really have a response. He was still perplexed. What just happened? - which Zipp voiced out loud at the same time coincidentally. He waited just a few seconds before he spoke in frustration.

"What the hell, dude? What's up Tripp!? Who was that on the phone? What's going on??!! He finally lost his cool, which finally snapped Tripp to here and now.

"Hey... Zipp... umm, I don't know what just happened. I was told my time is...*" Tripped jumped as he saw the wide eyed expressed on Zipp's face!!*

He reached for Tripp in an attempt to cover him.

"Watch out!!! That was the last thing said then there was darkness...

Chapter 7: The Call

Angel turned off her car and instructed the youth to make their exit snappy.

"And could someone grab my bibles? Both my KJB and my youth international version.

"OK, Mom, I gotcha." Melissa answered with a masked attitude. Ken hit his sister on the shoulder with a warning. They had a quick exchange of eye conversation. She rolled hers at him; however, she changed her attitude and put on a smile as she reached into the backseat armrest to retrieve the bibles. As the family got out of 2021.

Range Rover Sport everyone's eyes looked at the sky, noticing a quick and drastic change in the weather. Dark clouds were forming as traces of lightning crept across them. The sound of thunder rumbled in the distance, which caused the youngest of the family to grab onto his mom's hand in fear and need of safety." Angel squeezed the hand of her youngest with assurance. "What the.... where did this come from? "Andel said to herself but aloud "OK guys let's get a move on" she hastily ushered her family inside of the place they'd had attended church for the last eight years.

Ron released his mom's hand as he ran the short distance to the building, yelling over his shoulder. "Looks like we should have brought umbrellas," Lil Ron shouted over the rumbling weather as it started a light rain. The family all walked the last few feet to the church in a power walk as Ron held the door open for quick access.

"Thank you, Lil bro," Ken threw at his younger siblings as he unnecessarily bumped into them.

"Mom, Ron hit me." Ken whined even tho he, himself, quickly stuck his foot out, tripping his big brother in response to the minor assault. Melissa continued to roll her eyes at her brothers' antics, immediately remorseful with all she clearly had added to her mother's plate. And promising to herself and to God that she was going to be a better help around the house. Especially when it came to her brothers. She simply had to be a better example for her siblings.

"Really, Ron?!" I'm right here!! Don't let me deal with you right here in church?!! Tell your brother you're sorry... NOW!!"

"Sorry"... Ron muttered under his breath and Ken gave him a sneaky smirk, not wanting to receive his mom's wrath.

Angel let out a loud sigh. UURRGGHHH.. there are times that she wishes...

"Hey there Sis Angel", her thoughts were interrupted by Deacon Douglas.

"Good morning, Good morning, Brother Douglas. "

She greeted her brother with genuine affection. Deacon was the very person who received Angelica with open arms over eight years ago when she wandered into the church fresh off the streets. Ron was pre-k age and Melissa was still a baby and she was four and half weeks pregnant with her youngest son, Kenneth and was at her wits end with absolutely nowhere to go and no one to turn to. The young families were tattered and beaten and hadn't had a nutritious meal in a very long time. Every time Angel sought help, she was received with disdain and judgment. She was, at the time, heartbroken by the fact that she was going to have to give up her children. Deacon Douglas was "Brother" Douglas then. And even tho his position in the church has changed, she still addresses him as "Brother" Deacon and he made it clear that he was completely OK with it.

"Has my favorite church family doing this beautiful Sunday morning?" He smiled sincerely. "As a matter of fact, I'm glad I ran into you. Sis Sherry is a little under the weather, so she

won't be available to run the children's church this morning, and I was wondering if you could do me a small favor... he left the question fade away with a hopeful look on his face, But His question was interrupted with by a loud electrical sizzling sound followed by complete darkness.

Chapter 8: Confusion

As Darrel navigated the SUV down the road, he was completely in thought as to what transpired in the men's room at Benny's shop. Had he been daydreaming? Was the Incident really real? That couldn't be it. He recalled he had answered the phone as he entered into the men's bathroom at Benny's shop. Still, it was all so (unreal).

The only thing, tho, was how he felt in his spirit… in his heart. Something transpired that had to be accurate because… he knows he has changed. There was a change in him. All of a sudden, his life' passed by his eyes like a movie. In his mind, he went over all the things his father did. And as a result, he remembered all of the things he had done within the last … he couldn't even number the years because it had simply been that long... the lying, the sex with anybody, the sneaking around. The disrespectful attitude. Cheating on his wife, his QUEEN! Whom he knows he isn't even worthy of. He was blessed to have this amazing family. He once again knew where it all stemmed from.

His childhood. He also knew that if he hadn't become a part of ministry during college, there would be NO telling what direction his life would have taken. As He continued to muse, he was first overwhelmed with anger.. bitterness, and hurt. Growing up, his life was unspeakably despicable. Just tragic. When Chanel came into his life, in high school, she had no idea what kind of life he'd lived at home. Her and school became his saving grace the first way before he went to college. There were so many secrets he had hidden from his wife. Then guilt and remorse, even embarrassment, crept into his thoughts.

His eyes began to water as he realized he couldn't even begin to know how he was going to make up for his wife. To his friends. Oh my ... Benny! Who had been more than his barber? He was clearly the example of a father that he needed all these years but was too stupid to acknowledge. The caller said he was his, THE Father. That he knew him and was with him. Darrell thought it was his dad. What could that son-of-a bitch wants!! Wasn't he in prison or, more preferably, DEAD!?! Why didn't he just say who he was and what he wanted instead of all the games? He began to recall the Tumultuous childhood he and his little sister endured. The loss of their mom... the lack of food... roaches.. rates...no love.. just the abuse by the hand of their, if you can call him that, the hands of their dad.

His chess tightened when he thought of the unspeakable things that he and his sibling endured. It's been years since he had even allowed himself to recall the life their father forced them to live. All of a sudden, he felt something welling in his stomach and it was quickly making its way up his throat. He turned the steering wheel desperately towards the driveway of a nearby convenience store, almost causing a massive car wreck as he heard several sounds of screeching tires accompanied by profanity and threats.

It didn't faze Darrell as he opened the driver's side door just in time to regurgitate this morning's breakfast and last night's dinner onto the parking lot pavement. He continues to empty all of the contents of his stomach. To the point of gagging due to clearly having nothing left.

The angry rush hour drivers quieted down their rage once they realized what was going on with Darrell and reluctantly returned to their vehicles. One by one, the commuters continued on to whatever their destination was.

Chanel rushed over to her husband as quickly as her body allowed after initially being startled about what just suddenly happened.

"Baby, baby, Darrell, sweetheart, what's going on?" She asked, completely confused. At Benny's, he seemed just fine. He was his usual self, well... She did see a slight change in his mood once he returned from the men's bathroom.

He was still so occupied with whatever was going on with himself He didn't notice her noticing his drastic change. She was just about to ask him what was going on when it seemed as though his eyes were watering when suddenly they were off the road and in the parking lot. It was more than *a mystery. The sudden movement scared Chanel as she covered her pregnant stomach in protection of their unborn child.*

She gently patted him on his back, "Baby! Are you ok?" She spoke softly, not wanting to add any further stress to Darrell's current situation. She then waddled her way back to the car to grab one of the bottles of water they always had stocked in case of long commutes. That and healthy snacks. All because of her current condition.

"Here you go, sweetheart," she returned to Darrell, offering him the water. He looked pale even under his beautiful mahogany skin. She was very worried about him. Darrell is the picture of health. He had never gotten sick the whole time she had known him.

Not once. Even the very first time they met in high school. He stays in the gym almost more than at home. He eats healthily. Nothing added up, Chanel thought. She thought about his change of mood at Benny's, his quiet, solemn behavior during the drive, and even just a few minutes ago, him, at what seemed like, on the brink of tears... him getting sick! What's going on? For now, she knew she had to attend to her husband and his current condition, but she also needed to find out what was going on. They had a child on the way, and it was too late in the game for them to have a breakdown.

"Baby, rinse your mouth real quick, then take a few sips of this water." His breathing was ragged as if he had just run a mile. He grabbed the bottle of water, following his wife's instructions. He felt woozy as the tepid liquid traveled down his throat. Both he and Chanel jumped at a sudden "boom." They both looked up at the dark sky, as dark clouds

seemed to suddenly form. Chanel reached for Darrell just as there was sudden, complete darkness.

Chapter 9: The Accident

"What the hell!!" Zipp yelled as he looked up at the dark clouds suddenly appearing. Then He took a quick look at Tripp lying still on the pavement. He thankfully witnessed that Tripp lowered his arms which he instinctively used as a shield, so he was grateful Tripp seemed OK. At that moment, thunder permeated the clouds, and out of nowhere, it began to pour rain. "MAN!" Zipp jumped up from the position as a human shield that he had provided for Tripp, then, without a second thought, whipped out his phone using the voice app to contact the guys that were still in the club building.

He started running in pursuit of the perpetrators. Soon as someone answered, He barked instructions to get out of the club right now and get to Tripp and secure his safety as he pulled out his Glock and blasted several bullets at the retrieving black vehicle, which he recognized was a Mustang- Mach He was running as fast as he could in the pouring rain, towards the retrieving car as he continued shooting until he heard the empty click of his weapon. Zipp squinted his eyes, trying to see thru, the weather in an attempt to get the license information as he re-holstered his weapon. The car driver's reckless driving, coupled with the inclement weather, made it difficult to see more than the last two letters, well one letter, and one" number. "3B".

He repeated the information over as he turned and sprinted back to the spot where he left Tripp. He was both relieved and nervous that his close friend wasn't there. He hoped it was because his crew did what he directed them to do. He pulled out his phone, and once again, he used the voice app to call his main guy. The phone rang once before the baritone sound of Chuck (aka Charles) answered with a "Got 'em," signifying that Tripp was with them and he was safe.

"Cool. I'm heading that way. Hey, have IT taken to try and track down a black Mustang? I couldn't make out what year, and I was only able to get the last two details on the plate. 3B. And have her put legs on it, alright. I want this wrapped before the morning!" Zipp made it really clear that he wanted this situation handled ASAP! Whoever had the nerve!!... The disrespect!!! Yea they were going to be REAL sorry. This bad decision is going to be their last. Zipp jogged to the VIP parking section instead of calling the valet.

He was still hyped with adrenaline. He clicked the button on his key that unlocked his 1960 classic Corvette Sting Rey. As he sped out of the parking lot his mind was on the time he purchased his dream car. It was this first purchase when he and Tripp had made their first million with their business. Recalling that since they were teenagers that vowed to themselves that once they made it out of the tragic situation they were living in, the first thing they were going to 7C udo was buy the car of their dreams.

Tripp's was a vintage Mercedes 450 SEL 4.5- black. But trips were his beloved 1960 Corvette Sting Ray-red. The decision to purchase the vehicles was one of the things that had given the two young men any glimpse of hope to get out of their situation. They didn't have any "concrete plans of how they would achieve the outrageous plan, but the youth pastor at that time always said every decision had to have vision for a plan start. So, their plan was to get fancy cars. As he turned onto the block of Tripp's place, it made him chuckle at the minds of their young selves and how their lives were so completely different from how they raised us.

Well not completely, but at least they didn't have to worry about food.... and all of the other things that were happening around them and to them in their lives. He pulled up to the circle drive of Trips massive crib. Passing the other cars lined up along the curb, directly to the entrance double doors. He acknowledged the two men guarding the front doors with a lift of the head as he tossed his keys to the one on the right. He knew what Zipp wanted, and the gentleman caught the keys with one hand and then proceeded to Zipp's car.

He knew exactly the spot allotted to park the vintage man toy being that it has been his specific duty for the last few years. He also understood the assignment. There better not be not one scratch on the candy-red priceless vehicle, and no mud was allowed to be embedded within the tread of the tires. Even if washing the car was required. The whole thing may sound degrading, but the young man took pride in everything required of him. He knew once he started with the small things and knew he could be trusted, eventually, the big things would come.

Once the car was expertly parked into the tree, according to Zipp's instructions the gentleman returned to his position in front of the house. Zipp walked into the mansions conference room and notice the Tripp called all the fellas. So, there must be a meeting about the incident. As he walked into the great room, he saw everyone was present. Mo, John, Kalif and Chuck of course. "What's good?" Zipp greeted him as he walked right past his "brothers." straight to the bar and pored himself something to drink.

"So, what's the word?" He asked as he downed the liquid with one massive swallow. He placed the empty glass on the counter. He then made his way to his lounger; glad he didn't have to chase any poachers out of his spot. He wasn't in the mood for playing games.

He sat down and noticed how everyone was giving each other the side eye looking as they tried not to look at one another. Chuck shuffled one foot from the other in the corner of the room where he was standing.

As Zipp sat down he snapped, "WHAT!?" He said he then sat up straight was Tripp OK? He said to himself, alarmed.

"WHAT!?" He said even louder, pounding his fist on the arm of his lounger.

"Uugghh... umm, yeah, we just got off the phone with Buck (the only member of the crew not present). He found the driver and the people who were in the car..." he said hesitantly. Zipp bounced up from his seat. Pulling out his peace and bellowing to the members of his crew in the room. "What?!" He was impressed by how quickly his boys handled the situation. He seemed to just have hung up the phone with Chuck. He was glad they knew he meant business.

"So where are these punks?!Bring"emm here. Right as he finished his sentence, the door opened. Two young boys and one girl stumbled into the room evidently from being pushed by Buck. They were all crying. One seemed to have a busted lip from the evidence of blood on his face. Chuck took that time to inform Zipp of the obvious. *"Yeah... they're a bunch of kids."*

"Pleeeease!!!". The one with the bloodied face pleaded. *"We're sorry!* It was an accident! We didn't mean to hurt nobody. *Please, we are so sorry!!"* He cried to the room of men, clearly fearing for his life as well as the lives of the other two youngsters. As "a matter of fact, they were all pleading and crying!! "Too late for your sorry's young blood", Zipp said thru gritted teeth as he lifted the gun and pointed to the terrified youth. *"What crew you with?"* He said, directing the question at the injured young man. At the threat of getting shot he cried, *"I lost control of my car. And we had a couple of beers. And we were celebrating my new car and*

graduating, and my dad let us stay out, and we are sorry, so, so sorry. We would never hurt anybody!!"

You could barely hear the young man's pleas over the sobs of his companions. The other young man clearly had urinated all over himself and the young girl had cried so hard. She now was throwing up all over Herself. The three youths were beside themselves in fear. They were all coughing, losing absolute control of their faculties. Not concentrating on what would clearly be an embarrassing situation usually, the three continued to grovel and plead for their lives. In unison the three got on their knees, prepared to completely debase themselves and offer whatever it was going to take for their freedom.

Right at that moment, Tripp walked in thru the back entrance of the room. His eyes enlarged in horror at what he was witnessing. He looked credulously at Zipp with his gun drawn, the barrel zeroed in on three kids crying and pleading for mercy.

"WHAT IN HELL IS GOING ON!!!" He rushed over to Zipp. As he quickly reached out in an attempt to grab Zipp and lower his armed position.

"No Tripp. These are the thugs who tried to run us down at the club!" He concluded, No one was moved by the distraught youths. In unison again, the three said with teary eyes..." *THUGS?!!"* *The girl added "OMG!"*

"Man are you insane?!! Look at them", " he directed Zipp as he viewed the well and expensively dressed children who were now kneeling with clasped hands and heads down in prayer. "Have you lost your mind, man?! Can't you see they are not about this life!" He wanted to snatch the gun out of his right-hand man's fingers but didn't think disrespecting Zipp, especially in front of their whole cabinet, was a good idea. But he made a mental note to read Zipp his rights when they spoke man to man and this situation was resolved.

Tripp walked calmly to Zipp and lowered the arm holding the weapon. Eyeing him and waiting for Zipp to turn and look him in his eyes. After a few minutes, Zipp turned his vision slowly and gave Tripp a searing look. Letting him know how pissed he was that he had interrupted him while he felt he was doing what he was expected to do in this business. He was there to HANDLE SITUATIONS!! Good, bad. Right or wrong!! It was always his call. He'd deal with the carnage later. *"Stand down, bruh."*

Tripp once again admonished his old friend. Defusing the aggressive atmosphere. Even to his own surprise. This is not an isolated incident. They have delt with some of the most heartless, ruthless, cutthroat young bangers in the business. More than once. He's even lost a couple of his guys by the hands of the delinquents. But in his spirit, he knew this was not the case. Zipped leaned towards Tripp and mumbled thru gritted teeth, I'll holla at you about this later. He blazed a stare at Tripp. Leaving absolutely no question as to what he meant.

Tripp wasn't moved with his visual threat. He knew that everyone in the room knew what it was. His returning glare reminded Zipp to don't get it confused.

As he dragged his vision towards the three juveniles, he admonished them to stand up.

"Who are you?" His vision traveled from one of the young ones to the other.

"Say something", he encouraged someone to speak. His non-threatening countenance relieved all three and they all started talking all at once. "See, we", *"We got a chance to"*, *"We're sorry but"!*- In such a hurry to explain, everyone rushed in with their version of the evenings events not caring what the other one had to say.

Tripp lifted his finger to his lips *"Shhh"*, he quieted the three desperate children. Calming them down. *"It's OK. Just calm down"*. He looked around the room then directed everyone except Zipp, to leave. *"So what are you going to do?"* Zipp asked as he realized he was still on an adrenaline rush. Tripp gave him an extended glare as to let him know he needed to stand down. And to remind him who he was. The battle of wills went on for at least five minutes then Zipp leaned his back up against the wall in, not so much in a surrender but more like an understanding.

Trip flared his nose as he turned his attention toward the young guest, who seemed to recognize the line of authority and focused their attention on Tripp. They didn't exactly know who the new guy who entered the room was, but they read the room.

"And who are you?" He drawled the question to the youngsters. Feeling the drain of the past twenty-four hour finally catching up to him. Knowing that there was the type of shift that has happened or is happening. Whether it was a paradigm or spiritual shift, one thing he did know knew that a change had happened to him.

The young kid, with what is now dried blood on his face, spoke up.

"Uh, sir, um me and my sister and our cousin was celebrating our graduation and my dad surprised me with a car as a graduating gift and he usually doesn't even let us go anywhere without an adult or at least with our church youth group and he also let us stay out past curfew... the youngsters started tearing up again, "and my cousin snuck in some beers and I've never drunk before and I was driving and I got dizzy and... he paused.. sir I didn't see you and your friend" the tears found its way on the youngsters face and he couldn't finish.

"OK, OK, you can stop there." He gave Zipp another "Next time listen to me" look. Alright, does anyone of you have a cell phone? The second young man from the group scrambled in his ripped "New Religion" jeans almost dropping it as he fumbled it into Trips hands.

It was almost comical the way he tried his best to be respectful. Tripp smirked in fear of giving into the laugh that was girgling in his throat. He grabbed the phone, one that was exactly the same as the one he owned. Which confirmed his suspicion that the youth clearly came from a family with means. That and the new 2022 Mustang- Mach-E GT that almost mowed he and Zipp down like grass.

"OK, so, number?" He asked giving the young man a pointed stare. The young man's shoulders slumped as he realized Trip was calling his uncle, Pastor Wills! At that moment he thought it was almost better to have been shot!!... as he let out a shaky sigh. Trip gave the youngster another smirk understanding his trepidation. He dialed the number as the young man called out the numbers. Tripp put the smartphone to his ear just as an elderly gentleman yelled out..." Matthew!!?? ... is this you, Matt? The gentleman repeated in a frenzy.

Tripp's calm baritone spoke into the device.

"Sir my name is Tri.., uh Trever and it seems your kids partied a little too much last night. When there wasn't an immediate response he continued," I have to give it to them, tho, they pulled over and slept it off. I discovered their car against the curb right outside my home. I'm calling because they seemed to embarrassed to make the call. But they're just fine and I'll make sure they find their way home safely." He waited for the chain of questions he figured was going to come. It seemed as tho the man on the other line had left the phone or he was too relieved to talk ...then he did speak.

"You said...your name is... Trever?" came the weird response. Suddenly, Tripp had a quick moment of nostalgia. There was something familiar about the voice. Actually, the voice seemed to be one he had heard recently. He took a stab at the only name that the voice reminded him of God?

Chapter 10: Unanswered Questions

The sudden loud noise and darkness did more than catch Angelica by surprise. Especially considering how her day had started. That incident wasn't swept under the rug, not one bit, she just didn't know what to make of it. She knew God doesn't make house calls... well not by phone anyway. Then ...this. There was a fear that crept its way in the pit of her stomach. Where were her children.?!!

"Ken, Melissa, RonRon !!", she yelled out as she stretched out her arms trying to feel her way around in the dark hallway. "Mama!!" came the nearby frantic cries of her youngest son. She waved her arms desperately in search of her frightened baby boy.

"Ron, sweetie, don't move. I'm right here. You're OK. Ken!!, help me find your brother", She tried to hide the franticness in her voice. "Melanie sweetheart are you good? "She didn't want any of her children to panic but she took solace in the fact that she knew he daughter would keep her wits about herself. Even so., HER BABIES, HER BABIES!. What is this all about? Then right at the moment there was a sizzling sound reverbating somewhere in the walls, then, just like that, lights illuminated the building. What?! The electricity was off... that's what that was? She adjusted her eyes as she searched out her children which ironically where all lined up together on the opposite wall, just inches from one another.

"Man that was crazy". Ken said as he started to laugh. "YEA! It was like the haunted house that we go to during Halloween. All of a sudden Lil Ron decided he was fine with the darkness. "So immature", Melanie mumbled to herself thinking, "Surely I'm adopted", she chided as she switched sides of the hall next to her mother, rolling her eyes. "Everyone is ok?. Angel let out a sigh of relief. It was more a statement than a question.

Hey there, Watson family. Sorry about the power surge." Deacon apologized as he reentered the hallway. "Since they've be doing some construction across the street we've been experiencing those power outages at least once a week. "It's never been on a Sunday. "He pondered out loud, scratching his head. "I've made a complaint to the company and nothing has been done so far so I know to just head right to our breaker box. Problem solves. He shrugged his shoulders. "Is everyone OK?" He asked unaware of how the whole ordeal just put Angel in the craziest head space.

But she chuckled shakily deciding not to over think everything. Her kids where clearly fine. More than fine, so she just thanked God, put a smile on her face and turned to Deacon Douglas.

"Yes Brother Douglas we're fine. I think the kids want to do that again ". She ended with what she knew was a fake laugh. She did didn't enjoy that situation one bit. It kind of triggered so many things she had to endure in her childhood. Being suddenly encased in darkness was not what she would call a good time. Then a light bulb came on in her head. "Hey, about ne teaching children's church for today, I'd be honored ". She had a perfect subject to share with the youth of the church today. Today's incidents had her thinking about how real this life has gotten.

The children of today are so exposed to so much. By the age of 10 they've seen it all. There are absolutely no surprises!!! She felt that the direction things are going with today's youth is like a downward spiral. Social media's influence is crazy. So much so, that the thought of anything else hardly matters to the millennials and New Z's. Their phone is more to them than a phone to them. It's like their mother, father, teacher, best friend, husband and wife!! The definitely look at it more. She can safely say social media has become their "God"!

But how is she going to introduce her subject to the little robots? If the subject is not handled properly, she'd be rejected before her second sentence was even formed.

"I believe I have the right activity imma need some serious divine intervention so send one up for me", she gave the Deacon a playful wink and she ushered her family thru the hall to the foyer and ultimately into the church's modest Sanctuary.

By the bits of conversation and the confused look on the gathered individuals, they obviously were reeling towards the section where usually the youth congregated. She can tell they felt the same way her children felt about this mornings momentary scare by the animated facial expressions and the way they were using there hands while conversating with their peers.

"Perfect". She thought to herself. She asked for Devine intervention and that's what's she got. The youth seemed prime for this morning's conversation. "Mom can we go?" Ken asked clearly wanting to get in all the fum conversation that everyone was enjoying about this morning's black out. "Of course. But you know we'll start in... she looked

at the time on her Galaxy A71 5G smartphone, in about 10 min. Don't be back there clowning even if everyone else is!!

Remember after the morning announcements you guys' head downstairs to the basement for youth group. Spread the word".

Once the Deacon also found his way into the sanctuary,, she waved her hands to flag him down. The Deacon smiled as he walked over to Angel. "What can I do for you young lady" He offered. She has always been like a surrogate daughter and her kids were like his grandchildren. From the time he lost his beloved wife they have been like family to him over the years. He has filled on as babysitter to the children when she couldn't find childcare. Especially due to the night hours she had to work. When they first met he knew she was struggling and it was something or someone that lead him to simply be the support she and her little family needed. Eventually he recognized that they needed each other. So, anything she needed, the answer was always a "yes" from him "You and the kids ok?" He stated, referring to this mornings exiting escapade.

"Everything is just fine. Perfect, actually. Even tho it is usually customary for the youth to gather downstairs, at the fellowship hall, after the morning announcements, could you make sure their is a reminder announcement on it". She was clearly exited about whatever her plans were for the youngsters this morning and he was just grateful.

"Also, I know this morning's blackout was unexpected and definitely weird, but could you do me a favor?" She motioned for him to lean in a little closer as she whispered her instructions in his ear. He clap his hands and rubbed them together in excitement. He knew he had thrown this mornings youth session at her at the last minute and he was glad she took on the challenge with a willing spirit. He gave her a salute as if they were in the Armed Forces.

"Yes man", he playfully click his Kenneth Cole loafers together and hurriedly made his way towards the back of the sanctuary were the church offices were located to ask the church secretary to add youth group session to the church announcements. Time is winding down. "Great". Angel said to herself. Satisfied that this morning turned out unexpectedly what was needed. For the youth and for herself. She headed downstairs to the fellowship. To set up.

Due to the sound of footsteps coming down the stairs. It' was clear to Angel that the announcements had been read. She became more and more exited as she heard the noisy footsteps of the youth as they made their way into the fellowship hall.

Even tho this bunch were church kids the group was the still the average youth of today. Everyone walked with their faces in their cell phones. You had the few who were clearly the class clown. Then there were the "mean girls", the jocks, the nerds", the few "couples" who were on the precipice of discovering young love...which unfortunately she chided to herself, disappointment and heartache will mostly follow. The thought broke her heart a little. Just knowing that. But that is typically how it goes. She quickly wiped away the frown that formed on her face. Making that was a subject that was going to have to be addressed at another time.

She clapped her hands as she attempted to get the group to focus.

"Ok, guys. Settle down, settle down. Now, I know how important your phone are to you all but you also know the rules. I am completely sure you can survive the next couple of hours without "liking "or "unlinking" or "sharing" post' from your hundreds of friends on social media.

She made the quotation marks with her fingers which garnered a few giggles. She smiled at the fact that her little speech was moderately excepted instead of the opposite. She knew she was taking a wrist telling the youngsters to lower their "weapons" she chided herself again.

"Ok I have a question for you guys."... she purposely caused for effect. She surveyed the room making sure she had everyone's attention. After a few shook their heads and lifted their hands in anticipation and curiosity.

She continued. "Looks like I have everyone's attention". That statement was met with a few rolled eye and loud sighs. That's her when she knew she needed to hurry with her plan before she lost them. "OK. Has anyone ever burned their mouth on a hot drink? You know, tea, cocoa…coffee??

The question was met with a bunch of nodded heads, some "Yeps" and few "Heck yes"…Angel continued.

"I know, right. Ruins your whole day, right! Everything you eat becomes a challenge. And I don't know about you guys, but food is one of the main motivations for me to get out of the bed!". She was happy that that statement got a few laughs but there were mostly nodded heads of agreement. "Yes" she still had their attention. "OK, answer me this, has any ran a tub of water for a bath. You then just strip (laughter and a few whistles) she carried on, "Calm down, calm down", Angel said trying to keep the group focused.

"Like I said.. strip…then you just mindlessly jump in the water. With dreams of "bubble bath" happiness. Some "youuu tiiime", she dragged out the words once again for effect. Which was met with more nods, especially the young ladies.

"Cool. Cool. Well, you basically jump in with both feet dreaming of bubble bath bliss... then you quickly jump out in excruciating pain as you realize you forgot to turn on the cold water and you water's temperature was set on "HELL!". That one was met with a few "Awwww's". She quickly cleaned up her statement.

"I was referring to the extreme temperatures that the place "HELL" is understood to be. Anywho, how would you feel?

What kind of thoughts would go thru your mind? You can't get mad at anybody. It was your complete responsibility to check the water temperature. You wanna get mad. You wanna blame someone. But their is really Noone to blame. Nowhere to turn. You just made a bad decision. It's too late!! YOU have deal with it!!! You gotta deal the extreme heat on your flesh... HOW LONG IS THIS PAIN GOING TO LAST?!!!" Angel seveyed the room for any verbal responses...or physical reactions... She smiled as that question was met by some serious reactions. Their body language definitely showed that they were deep in thought.

"Good! I've got you thinking. Good, good, good!!! So...how long do you thing you'd have to endure the pain?

The whole room erupted with raised hands. A few verbal outbursts. She pointed to Tim on the fourth row.

"What do you think, Tim?"

"Well.. I'd call the fire department! The can use their water hoses on me" He said with all seriousness. Every laughed and someone thru a wadded piece of paper at the nieve youngster.

Lonnie raised her hand. Angel pointed to her. Lonnie looked at Tim with annoyance. "First of all the fire department couldn't do any thing about a scalded body, you need to go to the hospital so you

should call an ambulance". She finished with a satisfied smirk on her face. Angel corrected Lonnie. "Actually, you

CAN call the Fire department, Lonnie. Burn victims are their specialty. Remember they are first responders as well for any emergency situation so Tim is correct with his answer. But what could you have done to avoid getting burned?"

Hands went up again. With ferver!! It made Angel smile with satisfaction. They were thinking! She pointed at her son, Ken.

"Ken., what do you have to add?

"I think every decision you make has a consequence. So, you should be smart with your decision and thorough ". He ended

His answer with rolled eyed and someone disguised the word "Brown noser" as a sneeze which was met with more laughter.

Angel was proud that her son didn't seem to be bother with the hecklers. She met his defiantly glare with a wink and smile of approval. This made him smile. Angel continued.

"What Ken says is absolutely correct. And I don't say that because he's my son. Truthfully you should think of the long-term consequences of all of your decisions and actions".

That was met with someone disguising the word "Sure" as a sneeze. Then there was more laughter. Angel laughed as well. The group had to know she understood their mindset. Then she continued when the laughter died down.

"OK. We clearly understand that every decision has consequences. Good or bad. But there is one major decision that has everlasting consequences... (Pregnant pause- for effect) ... "So, if the thought of being scalded by hot water for just a few seconds doesn't sound like a good time, what can anyone tell me about... HELL... suddenly the room was enveloped in darkness.

No one moved.

"OKaay" Angel spoke tentatively but waited for something else to happen"

"I'm here" came a loud deep voice That made the room of youngsters errupt in screams out in fear!!....

"MAMA!!" Lil Ron's screams were the loudest....

Chapter 11: The Hospital

Chanel let out a loud groan!!! 'Now it decides to rain!! She hand her hands full dealing with whatever is going on with her husband, and I'm with a belly full of baby, no less, now a storm has decided to destroy the almost hour it took to perfect on her hair with what looks like a major rainfall forming that will wipe away any evidence of her mornings efforts.

The sound of Darrell retching onto the convenient stores' parking Lott reminded Chanel of the importance of what's currently happening with her husband. She turned her attention back to Darrell.

Rubbing his back and encouraging him to breath thru his nose between gags and not to hold back. "Let it run its course."

She reminded him that "she was there with him until the end and she would never leave him". And like magic he stopped! He spat out whatever residue left in his mouth. Rinsed his mouth with what was left in the water bottle that Chanel retrieved from their SUV. He straightened up from his bent over position and stared strangely at her like. Like she had just arrived.

His sudden glare at Chanel somewhat alarmed her. His behavior has just been weirder and weirder these last couple of hours. Like her happy, smilie, flirtatious husband has been taken over by emotional…distant…alien from another planet and it's causing her to look at him. I mean really look at him as he looked at her. His stare was frightening. Like he didn't recognize her. She was at a lost of words.

He was clearly going thru something and it hurted her not knowing what it was or what to say or what to do to help him get thru it. So there they were… looking at each other… "What did you just say?" Darrell looked as tho she were a ghost as he spoke barely above a whispered. As if he was a either afraid of what she had just said or afraid of what she was going to say next. That made it clear that he was really was going thru some kind of crisis and all she wanted to do was to hold him. To pray for him and with him and let him know that whatever he's dealing with, whatever is going on, they will get thru it together.

"Baby, I'm here for you. For whatever is going on. I'm right here. Always have and always will be. Ill never leave you baby. Never! But you have to tell me what's going on. You have to late me in." She grabbed his hand and pressed it against her growing belly. She had to bring him back to her. To them. To their little family. "Baby, what's going on? Is everything ok with us? Are you having second thoughts?" Tears began to form in her amber-green eyes. He and their baby are her life and the thought that he may no longer want to be with them left her ..lost! What was going on with him?" The thought just paralyzed her. Then at that moment their unborn child moved. It made the both of them jump. This is the first time Darrell had a chance to feel the life, that growing in his wife's stomach... move. And the timing was so right because the movement from his unborn child somehow jolted him back to Chanel.

He grabbed both of her hands and lovingly pulled his family to him. When she said that she would always be with him until the end and that she would never leave him, it was clearly a message, a reminder and it just became clear to him as to what he needed to do. He just folded them into the curve of his body. He saw the look on her face. And it hurt him to think that she would ever think that he would abandon her or his child. It just came to him that he never shared anything about all he has experienced as a child by the hands of his father.

Actually both he and his sister had lived such a tumultuous existence when they were young. He never shared it with anyone. Not even his wife or the members at church. Once he had a chance to leave that life he vowed to never turn back, look back or come back... EVER!! He didn't even know whether or not his sibling had excaped or even survived. It's been a long empty journey for him. Today's events had given him the strength to face the demons that had shaped him into the person he is. Today... but no more. Today, right now was going to be the start of something new. He pulled away from her and looked Chanel in her eyes.

The evidence of dried tears broke him. His beautiful wife. He had never actually looked at her. My God...God... she is so beautiful. He looked at her protruding belly. The baby decided at that moment to make itself known. As if to say 'Don't forget me!' Darrell chuckled and bent down and gave her stomach a little kiss. "Baby. My dear heart!! My beautiful wife ". He squeezed her as tight as he could without bringing either her or the baby any harm. "Baby, Baby, Baby!!! Just for just a few more seconds he just needed to hold her. He felt Chanel's body start to shake. He pulled away real quick and saw that Chanel began to cry. He felt heartbroken.

"Oh no Chanel, baby" he pulled her close again. "Sweetheart, don't cry.... I am so sorry, so sorry. You don't have to worry. Everything is just fine. We are going to be just fine, baby. I know you're confused. And I promise I'm going to share everything with you. Everything that has happened everything that's going on. But understand this", he pulled away from her again and looked her in her eyes... "Hey", Chanel wiped away the one tear that escaped. "Hey", he used his finger to lift her chin so she could read his love for her on his face.

"Chanel. We are ok. Today I experienced something... Inexplicable. But it made so many things so clear." He grabbed her hand and guided her back to the vehicle. "It was something that was so necessary", he continued, "Something that needed to happen so I can be the man and husband you and our child need.".

He helped her into the SUV and closed the door. Then he scurried on to the driver's side and jumped in, started the car and carefully made his way make it on the road to their home. Darrell took a quick peak over to his wife and noticed Chanel was looking intently out the window, deep in thought. Darrel reached over and grabbed her left hand with his right one. He intertwined their finger then leaned over to give her hand a quick peck. She looked at him for a couple of seconds. The look on his face was everything to her. A small smile crept it's way on her face. When Darrell saw those dimples, it was his undoing!!

"Yea baby we need to get home".

He pressed the gas petal a little harder but not too hard. He needed he and his family to make it home in one piece.

Darrell pulled up into their driveway pushing the button to the garage door. Once in the garage the door automatically lowered and locked itself. "Don't move" He directed Chanel as he jumped out from the driver side then closed his door. He jogged over the Chanel's passenger door. He opened her car door then stepped back a couple of feet to make room for her exit. He extended his arm to reach for her as he gently guided her out of the car.

"Ok baby. Take it slow. I got you." Chanel did her usual slide down the side of the high SUV seat as Darrell caught her assuring her a safe landing. The shift in him was so EPIC. He felt renewed. His commitment to life was now imprinted in his soul. He then had moment of heaviness when he realized the things he needed to do to make all of his crooked lines straight. To try and right all of his wrong doings.....yea it was heavy. But what was that that was said to him two Sundays ago. 'His yoke is easy and His burden is light...' yea he has this. It'll be a journey, actually a new path, a new walk. They made their way threw the garage to the side door that led to their beautiful home. He felt a little nostalgic as he remembered the day they walked into their newly purchased home.

At that time, Darrel was feeling a little proud of the fact that HE, a young man in his early twenties had bought such a "fancy" house in a "fancy" neighborhood. And it was their first time buying a home. It didn't matter to him that at that time, he had a frat brother who was the president of the bank that approved the loan. He still had to do the leg work. Come up with down payments, closing cost, title fees, etc. His thoughts went sour as he also remembered all of the women who contributed financially. So many women. Mostly older women but his indiscretions didn't have any respecter of person. He even tried men but that was a hard NO for him. As they entered their home he dropped his keys into the mosaic designated "key" bowl (his wives idea) and she hung up her rainbow colored Loise Vuitton hand bag. She headed to the bathroom, realizing she had forgotten her condition for a few minutes. Which was understandable in Lou of the morning's events, but her body was reminding her with a vengeance as she scurried to the bathroom.

Darrell was grateful for his wife's necessary pit stop. It gave him a few minutes to gather his thoughts and words as to the conversation that was about to take place between the both of them. After a few minutes, Chanel opened up the bathroom door and headed towards the direction of the stairs. Darrell stopped her with a wave of his hand signaling for her to join him in the family room. She was tired and needed a nap. Today had been more than enough drama for her. Anything else can wait. But Darrell seemed to be adamant. So, she followed his lead into her favorite room.

"Baby, I know you're tired but we need to talk".

"OK. What's going on?"

"Well, I don't know where to..., you know what, I'll just start from the beginning". He cleared his throat and paused to gather his thoughts. Ringing his hands he gave her that stare that had always melted her heart. He wasn't even aware of how much his presence just gave her life. Her love for him just completed her very existence. At that moment, He was just staring at her trying to find the words to begin. He decided to share the worst of him first. "OK. Chanel first understand you and our baby are my world. And I would never consciously hurt either one of you. I would lay down my life so you guys can have every good thing this world has to offer". He cleared his throat again. "But I've just been battling so many things physically, mentally as well as spiritually for as long as I can remember. I'm even suspicious that some things I've purposely buried due to the tragic content of the situations in my past life." Her expression of concern AND confusion compelled him to rush into his next statement.

"Baby, I killed someone."

Chapter 12: Caller Unknown

Not comprehending Tripp's response, the elderly man on the line repeated his question. "Did you say your name is Trevor?" Tripp didn't repeat his answer. Realizing he was not in his right mind. He was still confused about the call he received just yesterday!! Why does it seem like it was longer than yesterday', Trip thought to himself. If this was some kind of elaborate joke, there's going to be HELL to pay. Whatever the case, he just wanted some answers. Then he said to himself "NO" the call was real! He knew it! He felt it!! He was still effected by it. He knew his whole life had changed. What does all of this mean? He gave himself a mental shake and answered the gentleman's question.

"Yes, sir. The name's Trevor. And don't worry about the kids, I'll get them home safely, I assure you. Trevor held the line in anticipation of a response from the gentleman on the other end. "Well, thank you son..."

Even though He still felt like the voice on the lined seemed familiar He also felt as though the elder wanted to say something else. And He was correct. "Can I ask you something. You said your name is Trevor, right?"

Trevor was on guard. Why is the old man asking him what was his name?

"Yea, why?!" Tripp had a bit of trepidation in his voice. He immediately was on the defense. "Who are you?!"

The elder's voice sounded suddenly nervous "Sorry, Son. I'm a little frazzled. My Grandchildren's absence had me up all night. I don't mean any harm.

Thank you for helping. I appreciate it."

"Not problem." Tripp shorthanded responded then quickly disconnected the line.

The older gentleman still sounded like he had something he wanted to ask or say. Tripp just let it go. He slid his phone into his pocket as thoughts ran through his brain. He just needed to get these kids home and find out about the call he received yesterday. He was sure it was some kind of sick joke. But he wasn't laughing. He really wanted to get his people on it. But he knew he couldn't trust any one of his guys to keep their cool. And that wasn't the response he was going for. There's literally something about the whole thing that has him at his wits end. He's not the kind of person that depends on anyone for answers. HE was going to get to the facts. He just didn't know where to start. He dug in his front pocket to retrieve his phone. After unlocking his phone, he accessed his call log and scrolled back to the estimated time he thought he had received the call.

"Uuhhmm, uuhhmm." The sound of someone clearing their throat gave him paused. He looked over his shoulder at the reminder that the kids that were brought to his place were still there and needed to get home. But he wanted to get a jump on finding out who was behind the call. "Oh, yea, right, you guys are still here. We'll be leaving in just a few, I have a little business I need to take care of. Why don't you guys grab yourself some breakfast.

"Call Chuck". He spoke into his phone and Chucks phone rang.

"Yea." Chuck drawled lazily into his phone.

"Hey man".

"Yea". Chuck repeated with his typical laid-back response. Although, those who really know Chuck knew not to let the laid-back persona fool you. He was well respected in the game.

"I'm sending those kids your way. Get them some breakfast. Let them order whatever they want." "Got you, bruh". Chuck, in his usual fashion, asked no questions. He always just handled whatever needed to be handled.

"Thanks, bro." Even as the words exited his lips, Tripp knew there was a shift. 'THANKS'? What?! That word hasn't excaped lips ever! His life went from an abusive childhood to his current life, with, from his perspective, no one's to help!

Tripp didn't even have to see what he knew was Chuck's puzzled reaction to his wording. That is not his way of handling anything. He gave a command, it was handled. No questions!! No why's. No How's. NO THANKS!! This whole thing was blowing his mind. He just knew this "thing", this shift, was happening. He had no control. And that thought made him... perplexed. Not scared, NEVER SCARED!! He'll mentally yelled at himself. Tripp returned his attention to his phone. He, once again, accessed his call log and scrolled to the estimated time from the other evening. All numbers were those of business acquaintances except for the one "Caller Unknown". Now that his memory was jogged, he remembered being annoyed. He usually didn't even answer those unknown calls but something compelled him to do so that night and without any explanation life, as he knew it, will never be the Same.

Still investigating, He then accessed his voice call. "K". He commanded, referring to Keana, the head of his IT team, The line rang about three times before the sultry voice of a woman answered.

"What's on your mind, boss?" Jeana found it really odd to here from Tripp. Usually, his requests were relayed to her by one of his top guys. Things involving her department usually was too trivial for the big guy, so she couldn't wait to show him how important she and her "Tech team' was to the business.

"Yea, K. Can you retrieve a number from an "Unknown number" on my phone?" He went straight to the issue at hand.

"Well, I've never had too, but if you give me abiut an hour, I'm sure I can get that for you". She thought to herself, it'll probably only take 10 min but since this request is new. She'd rather give him tell a time that too long than too short.

"OK, hit me as you've got it, please."

He quickly hung up the phone. "PLEASE!!?" WOW!! He didn't have time to analyze his phone etiquette. All he could think of was the fact he'd be able find out who the caller was!

Meanwhile Keana was feeling surprisingly appreciated.

"He's not so bad" she mused then proceeded to get to work on the request.

She clicks on the high-tech device. She accessed the database to Tripp's carrier, the inputted all numbers connected to his number during the allotted time for that night. She then backed up her research by hacking into all cell towers database and cross referencing the time as well as the area of his location.

Once she had her answer, she dialed Tripp's number.

She hopes, her appreciated how expeditiously the situation was handled.

Tripp was sitting in his office when he git the called. He answered the line immediately. Almost before the first ring was done.

"So, what did you find!?" Was his urgent response. "Well, it looks as tho the phone was either a burner phone or perhaps a foreign line, but the trail goes absolutely cold. I hacked and crossed references to every possible network, cell tower... I'm telling you the person is untraceable... a ghost. Tripp just severed the line. He slammed his fist on his desk.

"O.K., Who are you!?"

Chapter 13: Brotherly Love

"Oh my Goodness!!!, MAMA, who was that!!" Lil Ron yelled clearly not enjoying the dark, now.

"OK, everyone. Calm down". She accessed the flashlight on her phone and several of her students followed suit.

Now, with phone flashlights sporadically illuminating across the room, the young group seemed to calm down a bit.

I'm right here. I'll be the in just a min", Came the deep voice again. "Don't worry my young friends I'll won't leave you in darkness." Fear grew with every word spoken by the mysterious voice.

There were a few gasps that surpassed fear, confusion borderline panic. Then the door that led to the fellowship flew open.

"It's only me." Deacon Douglas sauntered clueless unseemingly nit knowing the fear his voice evoked. Then the door flying open was almost everyone's undoing.

"Hold tight. I've got you". And in a blink the lights were finally back on.

The room was initially filled with a collection of sighs then suddenly it erupted into applause. There were a few "Whoo hoo's. And one young man shouted," you're the man DEAC!!", which garnered a few laughs.

As he entered into the fellowship hall, Deacon Douglas waved to the youth. Which encouraged more applause and "whoops" from the crowd. He and Angel shared a knowing nod and she gave him the thumbs up and he gave her an inconspicuous wink. Then he turned his attention back to the youth group.

*O.k. guys. Alright, the show is over." He added as he made his way to Angel. She gave him a grateful hug and whispered in her ear "Thanks Deac". He squeezed her arm in understanding of their little secret.

"You're welcome young lady. I better head back upstairs, remember we have that guess church visiting today and the Pastor has a few things he wanted me to take care of to accommodate or our guests." He gave her one last pat on the shoulder as he exited the room.

Angel turned her gaze back to the youth group.

"Sorry about that'll little hiccup guys, but we're back on track and we still have a little time to finish our discussion."

"What discussion. The lights went off before we could talk about anything ". Lonnie interjects with her usual "know-it-all" quips. But Ken protectively rushed in. "Nah, that's not the truth. We were talking about how hot Hell is then the thing with the lights interrupted us."

Ken said, looking at the group, then to his mother, letting her know that he had her back.

"Don't clown my mom!!! "He thought to himself defensively.

"That's correct, Ken. We WERE starting to talk about Hell then just like that!", she snapped her finger, we were in darkness. Just in a blink of an eye. BOOM!! No warning."

That's what the whole purpose of the whole exercise that she had planned with Deacon Douglas. It was so the young crowd could see how suddenly the end come happen.

She was grateful for Deacon Douglas' help. His impromptu voiceover was perfect for affect. She reminded herself to invite him over for Sunday dinner to show her gratitude.

She continued the conversation.

"Can someone tell me your first thought when the lights suddenly went out?"

All hands esthetically shot up, accompanied with some impatient "Ooo, Ooo'S". Wanting to give someone other than Lonnie or Tim a chance to respond, she pointed to Keala, who was sitting on the last row. Keala is usually very quiet because she is very shy. So, Angel really was interested in what the young lady had to say.

"Keala, what are your thoughts?" Angel encouraged the young girl. She felt very happy that everyone seemed to be engaging in today's topic and for Kim, who pretty much just observes with not so much as a peep, gave her a boost that had not expected, but welcomed non the less.

"Well, we were talking about the devil, then the lights went out all of a sudden, and that voice said what it said. I thought we were all going to hell right then." Keala's voice trailed off as Angel saw the little girl visibly shrank back into her little shell. Even the look on young ladies' face showed that she was just as surprised at herself for voicing her opinion.

Angel gave her a big smile then focused her eyes on the rest of the kids.

"WOW. That's interesting. Did anyone else feel the same way?" She questioned.

There were a few mumbles, and it seemed, a few sidebar conversations were being held as well.

"If, what Keala said was initially what ANY of you felt when the lights went out, raise your hand".

The group looked at each other, giving so,e eye conversations. They were all waiting for some to respond first. Then one by one the hands went up. Until all hands were raised. All except her son, Ken and her daughter Melanie. They probably knew what their mother was up to. And the smirks displayed on their faces, confirmed her thoughts. HER eye conversation with them said, "DON'T GIVE ME AWAY PLEASE." And after briefly looking at each other then back to her, they "eye conversation" her their cooperation. With that, she gave a quick smile as to say thank you, then turned her attention back to the students.

"Humm... you thought we were in hell? Was her question.

Lonnie raised her hand as she spoke, rudely not waiting to be called.

"I think the fact that we were talking about ...H. E DOUBLE HOCKEY STICKS (she spelled out the word), then the lights suddenly were off. I just think it was just on our minds. We couldn't actually be in ..." she paused... "that place cause it wasn't hot. But still it was a bad feeling". Lonnie finished.

Angel was proud of how intuitive the young lady was. She wanted to get some more opinions. She pointed to John.

"John what's your take on what just happened?"

"I agree with Lonnie, but I was feeling the same as Tim was feeling at first and I was scared". His thoughts were met with lots of nodding heads, yep's" and some even a few, *"That's what I felt"* came from the majority of the room.

"Well, that is really interesting. Very interesting."

Angel paused for a minute. She wanted the group to grasp the implications of their thoughts. She also weighed her words on her next question.

She affectionately looked over the bunch and her heart swelled with love but at the same time her heart was heavy. How could she shift their priorities from wanting to get "likes" on social media or taking selfies, to consciously being more concerned about the destiny of their lives. She wants the session to be interesting but more than anything, it has to be more important for the whole room to take this subject seriously. She's never been the preachy, preachy type. She wanted everything she shared to be relevant to their everyday lives. She just believed in walking the walk. And helping the youth to navigate through the hurdles and darts, that are sure to come their way. And it may very well be the reason they can LOSE their way. She was totally a witness Angel soberly thought to herself. The subject was a BIG one, but in Lou of a certain phone call she that recently received, she knew she didn't have neither the time nor the patience for foolishness. She needed to be real with them.

So, Angel decided to just bite the bullet and go for it!! "So where do any of you think you're going be, forever, after you leave this life?"

That question was met with wide eyed confusion. Seeing a few startled expressions, she wanted to continue to keep the momentum.

"If the last hour of our morning shook you. How would any you like for it to actually become your reality?"...once again... HEAVY!!

"I just wanted you all to be conscious of what we talk about here in a youth group. I'm not the usual facilitator. So, I wanted my time with you to really make an impact on you all.

After seeing the class visibly exhale, she decided to lighten up and just leave her question something for them to ponder.

"Anyways!!! We all know hell is hot, but ice cream is cold!!! Can anyone tell what their favorite flavor is?!!

The shift was sudden for the group, but it didn't take them long to make it. Immediately hands were up as favorite flavors were shouted at her. She was grateful again that she was able give them something real and important to think about. But she also needed them to remember they were still children. She motioned to two of the older children of the group to help her grab the tubs of ice cream as well as some bowls and spoons in the kitchen. That seemed to do the trick. Everyone's whole demeanor went from introspective to IN NEED OF SUGAR!!!

As she walked through the kitchen door she almost collided with Deacon Douglas.

"Oh goodness Brother Douglas, we almost had a car accident, she chuckled as he balanced the tray of crystal glasses and bottles of water.

Lol, I know. I was just getting our guests some water. It looks as though the head pastor was caught up with some kind of issues with his grandchildren so the associate pastor, a uh Pastor Wilmar Lawrence, I believe that's his name. Hey, you guys have the same last name. Anyway, he's new to their ministry. A transfer, I believe. He continued as he made his way upstairs to the sanctuary. He didn't notice the startled look on Angel's face.

The teens also almost collided into her as they were entering into that church kitchen directly behind her.

"Oops, Sis. Angel, my bad." The one of the young gentlemen apologized as he and the other teen walked past her and gathered up the items for their treat. They also didn't notice the almost panicky look on her face after the Deacon spoke to her about their guess before leaving the kitchen. They just simply did what Angel asked them to do, of course between jokes and jabs at one another about the cutest girl in the youth group. They grabbed the ice cream, plastic bowls and spoons, then returned to the youth group.

Meanwhile Angel was paralyzed.

"Wilmar Lawrence...it couldn't be the same one?" She began to shake uncontrollably. She looked around. She quickly remembered the other room fill with young people... she told herself to just breath. It might not even be the same one. Then thought, "But how many Wilmar Lawrences', could there be living here in the same city". She calmed herself, remembering once again of the large group of youngster waiting for he just in the next room. Her mind stayed on name, Wilmar Lawrence. Her church's visitor. Which were just upstairs. If it was him, she wasn't sure how to handle it. It's been years since she had even spoken to him. Remembering all went down, she thought, "Wasn't he dead?" Wilmar Lawrence....? She put her hand over her mouth to muffle her voice as it broke... "Oh my God...Dad?

Chapter 14: Ringing Phone

When Chanel first came into the room, she was so tired She had settled her body into a lounging position on the love seat, but Darrell's words had her sitting completely erect!

"Wha... you did what?! WHY? WHEN?!! What are you talking about Darrell!

They had been together since high school and she does not remember him getting into any trouble with the law. He had been a model "A" student. A favorite with all the teachers. The only time they were ever apart was when he had to keep his eyes on his sibling, or he had to work.

"What do you mean, you killed someone?!" Chanel repeated her question.

"Baby, it was a very long time ago. It was before high school. Before you and I ever met." He waited for more questions. He was ready to finally unload this burden that had plagued him for most of his life. He and his younger sibling had lived an unspeakable existence. Sexual abuse. Child trafficking. Imprisonment. Every lack you could think of was the story of their life.

But now that he has spilled the worst part of his story, he was tongue tied as to where to go. Then he decided to go as close to the beginning that his childhood mind would remember.

His eyes glossed over as he traveled back to his childhood. Before he uttered a word the tears began to form in his big, beautiful mahogany eyes. Chanel leaned forward to hold his hand that also seemed to be shaking. What is going on? She used her left hand to stroke his well-groomed bearded face to show him she's right here. And whatever he had to share they will get thru it. As God as her witness.

He reaches up for her hand and clasped them together. He brought them to his lips and kissed both of her hands then patted them as he placed them in her lap. He sat up straight as he gathered the strength to share his life's story.

"Baby...". he paused, took a deep breath the forged on, "when I was a young boy, I believe I was either nine or ten, my mothered died. Actually, she was killed by my father." Chanel covered mouth as she took in a short breath in terror.

The mention of his mother was his undoing. He begins to cry. His mother. His beautiful, kind, strong loving mother. He hadn't realized that thos was going to be so hard. But he wiped the tears with the back of his hand. Chanel interrupted and reached over to their lamp table a grabbed several pieces of Kleenex.

"Take your time, sweetheart. Take all the time you need." She just needed him to know that whatever "this" it's just going to ok. They were just fine. Darrell sniffed the went on.

"It seems he found out that she had whole other family that lived right there in the same city where we lived. Well, I don't think you can officially call it "family", she had a child tho, a son to be correct." Once he began, he knew he was committed.

"It seemed as tho he had been having her followed by a a Private Detective for months and when he finally got proof he snapped. The next day of his discovery, He followed her himself. It's said that she would visit the boy every evening when she got off work which explained why it took her so long to get home. She always blamed it on traffic. We always had either takeout, leftovers or a late dinner. It didn't bother us kids, but it made my dad suspicious and that's when he hired the P.I. He claimed that he was following her to catch her and confront her. When he arrive to the house tho, she saw him hugging a man as a child stood at opened screen door... smiling... clearly expecting her. He took off in a rage a headed back home. I remember when he arrived. He rushed up the driveway, slamming on the brakes. He slammed the car door when he got out, so hard I thought the windows were going to shatter. " He leaned back on the lounger he was sitting on and continued.

"We kids didn't know what was happening. We didn't know he was agree about our mom. I figured something had happened at his job. My sister hurriedly ran upstairs to her room and closed the door. I already knew she just wanted to stay out his way. I wanted to Stay out of his way too, but something inside of me kept me downstairs.

Although I was hidden, or at least my dad was too enraged to see me. Which was probably a good thing. He never really needed a reason, so he hit us. He was always angry. Forr what?... you name it. We were talking too slow, or laughing too loud, did do our chores food enough. He was an angry man." Darrell took another big breath. "I haven't thought about these things for so long, I'm amazed that I can remember everything so well. The details... he was always...just...never satisfied." He then paused for a very long time. Almost like the memories were really too overwhelming to go on.

Chanel wasn't going to rush her husband. She also had to take in the horrific story he'd been sharing. It had to be the hardest thing for him to recall all of the despicable things from his childhood. She wanted to sit right next to him but when he leaned back into the lounge chair he was sitting in, that told her he needed his space for now. Then suddenly he continued.

"Anyway, when my mom arrived, he rushed out the door that was connected to our garage. I guess he wanted to meet her as she pulled in. She never even made it inside the house. He just started in on her immediately. Accusing her of lying. I know I heard him hit her." His eyes teared up. "She first asked him, "What was wrong? What did she do? He yelled at her about sleeping around. About their whole marriage, while he was out there busting his butt to provide for his family, she was neglecting their kids a ...whoring. Darrell's heart was visibly breaking.

Chanel leaned over to grab his hands. There wasn't Chanel leaned over to grab his hands. There wasn't any word to say so she just wanted him to know she was there in love with him. She silently cried for her husband. She cried for the little boy whose childhood was interrupted...stolen from the one person who should have protected him.

"It wasn't true. My mom was an amazing mother to me and my sister. Loving, caring. Always laughing. She had jokes for everything."

You can see the love he had for his mother in his eyes. Chanel's heart then began shattering. "They fought. I heard you try to explain. She mentioned that she was raped before in her teens and a child resulted from it. The child, her son, was being raised by his grandparents. The guy he saw her with was the child's grandfather. He didn't believe her... He closed his eyes as he described what he heard. "I didn't know what was happening. I heard what sounded like her choking. I heard her whimpering. I was frozen in fear. I wanted to help Her...

Well eventually the yelling, fighting stops. I didn't even hear her whimpering any longer or the choking. That's when the flood gates broke. He couldn't hold his sorrow any longer. And neither could she. She rushed in and held her husband. Her strong, manly, compassionate beautiful husband. He never showed sadness or weakness or vulnerability of any kind during their whole relationship. Even when they were in high school. My God, what he must have been struggling with... to keep up the facade. He was a model student!!

"I knew he killed her. I knew he did. It took him a really long time to come back into the house. And when he did, she wasn't with him. He rushed upstairs then came back down with blankets. I didn't make a sound. Man... my dad had just killed my mom. I was lost. I scared out my mind... then I was angry... I wanted to kill him!! I wanted to grab my sister and leave!! But I was ten. And my dad just killed my mom...

He was quiet again. He leaned back in the chair again with his eyes closed. Time passed. Then he fell asleep. She knew he was both physically, mentally exhausted as well as emotionally drained. She grabbed the throw from the couch and covered him. She just let him sleep. He can finish his story when he wakes up... that is if he wanted.

Chanel knelt down next to Darrell. "God, please speak to me. Tell me what to say to sooth my husband's broken heart". She rises from her kneeling position to kiss her husband on the forehead. She turned off the side lamp and laid down on their couch. She knew sleep was going to be impossible for her. So, she just kept an eye on Darrell. She knew his story was just beginning.

Chapter 15: The Gurney

Tripp had to take a breath. He was over thinking this whole situation. The caller didn't call back. The world is still the way that it's always been. Nothing has really changed. Then he had to detract that thought. Something has changed. He has changed. He then thought of something else that could have happened. He's heard about people using hypnosis to control other people's minds. Yea! That's probably what happened. But if that's the truth, what next?

The sound footsteps interrupted his thought and the kids from the other night walked in. They seemed to have made themselves at home. Chuck walked in behind the tree.

"They ate", was all he had to offer. Then he turned around and walked out of the room. For a second or two there was an awkward silence as the three waited for Tripp to tell them that he was taking home.

"Alright guys" let's get you home". Wait?! Here he goes again. Why is he taking them home? He has plenty of people that he employs to handle things like this. Still, He got up from his chair. As he made his way around his desk as the one named Mathew spoke.

"Excuse me, Mr. Trevor..."

"Just call me Tripp". He pulled out his cell phone and spoke into it.... call Chuck he accessed his voice call app. He looked at Matt to motion for him to finished whatever was going to say. Yea, uh...my grandfather called back and ask if you can drop us off at the church?"

"Church?!. Okay, alright. Yea. you guys are old enough that I don't have to walk you in or anything.. ok guys let bounce". He led the kids to the front where his 2022 Range a Rover Sport was just being pulled around. He gave the small group a few riding rules as they climbed into the luxury SUV. It had all of the bells and whistles. The seats had their own individual heating/cooling system. Matt and his family were almost tempted to touch all the buttons......ALMOST. Tripp made it clear that the rules were written in granite.

Tripp doesn't even know what the point for any rules was, no one ever rode with him in that particular vehicle. Both this one and his vintages Mercedes have priority in his life.

Everyone buckled up their seat belts and sat as respectfully and quiet as humanly possible. "OK, what was that address again?"

Tim gave him the church address that his grandfather ask them to be dropped off at. Tripp can tell that the little youngblood had an attitude. He can imagine the conversation that he the older guy had. He laughed at himself. Little Dude still didn't know how fortunate he was to have someone to even care for. It had been a while sense anyone cared about his whereabouts unless it involved getting or giving money.

Tim was actually mad at his grandfather. He thought, "Why couldn't he just simply let him drive his new car home so they can at least shower and change clothes before coming to church instead of looking like they currently looked. He still didn't know how blessed he and the other two were. They were wearing New Religion and Gucci. The latest Jordan's. Any child would love to be stuck wearing what they were "stuck" wearing. Tripp just shook his head. He'll get it one day. Well, he hoped so.

They headed to the destination in silence. The three were sulking about not having a chance to freshen up. Tim sulking about being grounded from driving his car that he literally just got. Tripp still just wanted to know who the unknown caller was that has turned his world upside down. And the fact that he's pulling up to the church house has him feeling a certain way. He hadn't darkened a church house doorstep in years. And the time he did go to church was a lifetime ago. When he lost his mother at the age of 11, he'd never forgiven God. And when he thinks of how crazy he had to be to think he can be mad at God. He was just heart and lost. He was so sad. His mom was the best mother anyone could have even asked for. She was loving and funny and funny and... he hadn't thought about her in so long he'd forgotten how it always made him feel. He cleared his throat not wanting his passengers to know what was going on with him. Really... what WAS going on with him... he really wanted to know.

They pulled up to the church. And, due to the lateness of the morning, the parking lot seemed to be full to the brim. Tripp was impressed as to how many people even still come to church. There seems to be so much misery and evil everywhere in the world. He had a modicum of guilt knowing that for years he had contributed to the madness. He did whatever he could do to fill the void in his life. And he knew he rolled over any one in his way. He never thought about God... until the call. By the way, if all God is doing is calling folks on the phone and causing confusion, it's no wonder why everything is completely messed up.

His mind went back to how his mom always talked to him about how loving God is. And how he watches over everyone. And how he provides and protects everyone. Then she disappeared!! She never called. She never said goodbye. And that just let him know that all the "God" stuff was a lie!! Fairytales!! Actually, church is just a big business. And from the looks of it, business is going good! He rolled up and down the parking Lott aisles. "Hump, I might need to speak to someone at the church! He thought, maybe he should talk to Tim's Grandfather about a partnership. While trying to find a parking spot, he heard the sound of music coming from the building. It sounded like a concert more than Sunday Service.

Looks like "Club Church' is LIT!!

After rolling thru every aisle and realizing parking wasn't going to be an option this morning, he informed his young guest that he'll just drop them off at the door, but to make sure one of them called him to make sure they were cool. Tim pulled out his phone and hurriedly imputed the numbers as fast as Tripp called them out. As the kids were exiting out the SUV, the upbeat song that Tripp heard coming from the church earlier, ended and the band was starting a new, slower... oh man!! He recognized the intro of the next song. It was actually one of the songs he'd heard his mom humming and singing around the house. She sure could sing. Living with her was like living in a concert hall.

Trip shook his head, snapping out of his fevered at the sound of the kids saying their goodbyes. He nodded his head in response, but he couldn't shake this feeling. The same feeling he's had since "the call". He just came to his mind that some of what he has been feeling was fatigue. He was tired. Tired of always having to be "on" every minute of the day. Always having to be in front, always being the boss, making sure to not get close to anyone, never letting anyone in. If truth we told he doesn't really enjoy... much of anything. He really hasn't experienced love.

The last person he knew who loved him...was. Before he even said her name he put his head on the steering wheel. It was from exhaustion and also there was a fresh wave of heartbreak consuming his sole, about his mother. Even tho she just "disappeared" from his life, his love for her never diminished. And then for some weird reason his mind traveled to his dad. He remembered when he found out how he was conceived. It seems like tho his life was destined for hardship. After his mom's disappearance, he had a really hard time.

Even tho he grew up living in his grandfather's home. They were never really close. To him Tripp was a just a product of his son's bad decision. His grandfather only softened up because Tripp's mother's loving and forgiving spirit just won him over. It tortured him, known his Dad was an abusive addict. Who did whatever he needed to do to get high.

Including robbing and raping his beloved mother. He doesn't have any real memory of the man. Just his face. And that was due to a faded picture his grandfather had stuck by a magnet on their refrigerator. He remembered his father was found dead in some crack house. This was when he was around the age of one or two. Inspite all of the sketchy history surrounding the people who raised him. He was still grateful for the woman he could affectionately call mom. And as the song, that reminded him so much of her, clearly was coming to an end, he still was eternally grateful for her. He was teetering between finding a parking spot and going inside or just pulling off and saying goodbye to the whole issue, the kids, the grandfather, the song... the whole situation, he heard someone burst through the church front doors. It was some woman who bent over. He couldn't clearly see if she was crying or throwing up because of a gentleman who rushed out right after her. He looked like he was attempting to help the young lady. Someone else walked out of the church front door. That's when he saw "Him" ... He was older but his grandfather showed him pictures and that face was forever burned into his brain. It was the face of the person he was absolutely sure was responsible for the disappearance of his mom! Without a thought, Tripp pulled out his gun and with determination jumped out of his car and made his way towards the small bunch standing at the church entrance. And at first glance it seemed as tho they all may have been in the midst of some type of heated discussion. That just hyped him up more!

The timing was perfect. The stage has been set just for him. He thought how ironic it was that God says that you should not kill. That's too bad because right here, right now, that very commandment was about to be broken. Right on GOD'S front door...

Chapter 16: Until the end of time

Chanel stirred when she heard Darrell moving from the lounger next to her that he'd fallen asleep in. She pulled her phone out of her shirt pocket to look at the time. WOW!! They have been asleep for almost three hours. Darrell rubbed his eye trying to wipe away the evidence of the morning's emotional events in addition to sleeping in his eyes as well as the embarrassment of baring his sole to his wife. He literally opened up a pandora's box when he finally told her everything that he'd been keeping hidden from her their whole relationship. Well, when he thought of it, he'd only shared with her just a fraction of the horrors he'd experienced as a child and teenager.

"Hey handsome." Chanel opened up the conversation tentatively. Not knowing how he was feeling. She could only imagine what was going on in his mind.

"Looks like We had a much-needed nap". She continued. Now that she's fully awake, their last conversation is hitting with force. His dad seemed to have ...killed his...mother.!!!?? What person keeps that kind of secret without having completely lost their mind. She realizes as much as she loves her husband. She's suspicious that she doesn't really know who he is. What kind of life did he have to endure. And his sibling? His sister?!! She never asked about her and he didn't volunteer anything regarding her...until today.

She was at a loss for words. How could she express how much she loved him even more without him thinking or mistaking her emotions for pity. It amazes her how he had conquered the unimaginable and at such a young age. This revelation explained so much. There were times she'd caught him so lost in thought that it seemed as though he wasn't even in the room. She figured it was a "man" thing. She knew surely being the head of the head of the house was serious responsibility and Darrell did not take its lightly. So, his times of "spacing off" were legitimate to her. And now she wondered how many times was him just in remembrance of his troublesome childhood. Darrell stretched and yawned. His actions were more so to prolong the conversation that he knew had to be finished.

Chanel knew he was still struggling with all he shared earlier. He seemed as tho that was just the beginning. And even tho she wasn't really ready for the rest, she had to be there for her husband. In her mind she knew that if she was struggling with simply hearing the things he was sharing, she couldn't even fathom having to not only experience it but to have to relive it over and over. Especially during times today.

Darrell knew he had to finish what he started. He knew the time for healing was finally hear. But his mind went to other things going on in his current life. He was pondering the due date of his child, which is literally any day now. He remembered that his church had been invited to a affiliated church's celebration tomorrow and he wanted to get there early to speak to the Deacons and give out instructions. He was thinking of why he was such a perfectionist. He admitted to himself how much of a control freak he was. How he had been existing a life of lies and manipulation. Realizing that he was slowly turning into his dad. If he hadn't received that mysterious call from... well whoever, he wouldn't now be experiencing what he realizes is a serious and necessary wake-up call.

He straightened up and cleared his throat. He rubbed his eyes once again. This time it was so he could have a clear view of his beautiful, amazing wife. This next part is going to be more difficult than he wanted to admit but he can't stop now. His marriage meant the world to him. Chanel and his child are his world. Today he intentionally will be healed.

He moved to the love seat which his wife had fallen asleep on, then leaned forward and grabbed both of Chanel's hands and drew her as comfortably as her swollen midsection would allow. He knew everything she shared with her was very heavy. It was a lot to take in. She was probably still trying to process the information. He knew it was asking a lot of her to understand who he was and know that he is getting better and stronger second by second just because of him finally getting a chance to clear so much up. It was a burden. More like an albatross chained around his heart.

The Mask he'd been wearing started smelling a long time ago he'd just become nose blind and no longer recognized the rottening stitch. It moves away from smelling to slowly suffocating him. He'd been existing above water for so long he felt like he'd been floating in an ocean of pain, bitterness and regret. But today he has stood up! He recognized that the water was just only two feet and he was never in danger of drowning he only needed to stand!!! Move forward. One step at a time. Even if the steps were baby steps, he just needed to move forward leaving the past behind. He needed to press for something greater. Both literally and spiritually.

"Baby, you've been staring at me for about ten minutes but I'm suspicious in thinking your eyes were looking at something else." Chanel spoke softly, not wanting to jolt Darrell from wherever he'd been these last few moments since the moment they'd awakened from their afternoon rest. *"Yea, I was just gathering my thoughts. Sifted thru some rough memories, trying to find the words to move forward without scaring you away."*

"Scare me away," Chanel lifted her right hand to cradling his handsome, dimpled chin. Thinking to herself that her husband had to be the most handsome man on the planet. He also had the biggest heart. That is what really attracted her to him. Looks will always fade but his loving heart and his positive personality has only made her continually fall deeper in love with him. And that there's is not one thing in the vast universe that could make her ever leave him. "Baby, this is us. Don't you know by now that you are imprinted on my heart. That whatever comes our way, whatever past, present or future trials or Triumphs, we'll get thru it... together.

Darrell continued to look her in the eyes, hoping that what she said was real. She is just too good to be true and he is forever grateful that God allowed him to find her. Especially considering the things he experienced in his youth. His mother was never to be seen after that horrific night. His dad's excuse to anyone who asked about her whereabouts was that she abandoned the family. His dad was a very upstanding man in the community. No one knew of his abusive side except for his wife and children.

He could charm the fangs out of a Cobras mouth mid bite. Thats when Darrell knew that that's where he got his manipulated, persuasive personality from. And he also admitted to himself that he was also, physically, the spitting image of his dad. The same built. Same height. The thought angered him. He didn't want to be anything like his father. The thought broke his heart. He remembered how life with his dad was. He vaguely remembered feeling so he happen to hear the sound of his dad's car as he returned from home. He'd pick him and my sister up always at the same time. He is on the right and his sister on the left. To Darrell, his dad seemed to have the strength of a thousand men.

He remembered his dad telling him that the reason he was always picked up with his right hand because he was his right-hand guy. His heart simply sank. He did remembered that for a short time of his childhood he lived a great life with his family...were really, really happy... then came his mother's secret... that was when their lives had taken such a dark turn. His dad just became...angry was not even the word. His conversation with the whole family was ...what was the right word. HATEFUL! That was it! He, just like a little boy, didn't know what happened. What happened to his hero. His dad... and why did he and have to kill him.

Chapter 17: The Emergency

Angel mentally and physically gathered herself. She wasn't going to allow the mere mention of the name to rattle her. The last time she laid eyes on him he was laying lifeless in a puddle of blood at her childhood home. She remembered the day like it was yesterday.

She and her brother were just talking in his room. He was packing and preparing to head off to college. He was giving her instructions. His plan was to get settled and stable in his dorm room. Get to know the layout of the campus and the dorm mother or brother's schedule. His plan was to take her with him because there was no way he'd leave her with that madman they unfortunately called Father.

Here lately Darrell notices the way his dad stared at his younger sibling. He knew what that look meant. He'd heard all of the horror stories of widowed fathers. Of how their demented sick minds felt that their daughters should take the place of their diseased wives as the "woman" of the house. He also knew if he ever laid one hand on his sister in that way, without a second thought he would end him. He had already gone to blows with him when he thought he was going to take a belt to her just because she called herself having a little male friend. Or "boyfriend" as she called the poor unsuspecting joker. Darrell knew that bringing anyone into this house of horrors was something liken to prison or just HELL and their father was Saten. That would have to have been considered the cruelest, sickest joke. And no one deserved to be exposed to their father. Not even their worse enemy.

Angel was also sick to her stomach when he shared what he'd been suspicious of about their dad. So, from that day they began to plan.

They heard the sound of their dad's car pulling into the garage. They both sent up a quick prayer then crossed their fingers hoping that he hadn't stopped at a bar and had a few drinks. Whenever he was drunk, he found everything under the sun to put his hands on one of them. They usually just stayed locked in their rooms and stayed out of his way until he fell asleep. It usually worked most of the time but not all of the time. And at the sound of him bamming on her bedroom door, that was not one of those times.

He banged and shouted well rather, slurred her name. He was telling her to come sit with him and keep him "company "in his bedroom. When he didn't get any answer outside of her room, he stumbled his way to her brothers room bamming even harder. She knew he was angry at her ignoring his request. Which she always did. She knew that eventually he'd pass out but today he seemed to be adamant. It was as if he was the big bad wolf, huffing and puffing. Darrel just couldn't take it anymore. He snatched his bedroom door open and gave their dad the hardest glare. It seemed have worked.. for just five minutes, tho.

Then his right hook connect to Darrel's chin knocking him back into the room. He lunged at Angel slurring and spitting his demands. She was supposed to provide him with what their "whore" of a mother freely gave to some other jerk. So, it was her responsibility to keep him happy. Angel was horrified. She tried to break loose from his death grip, but he was just way too strong. Even in his inebriated state. She started crying hysterically for her brother to stop him. And her brother didn't waste any time. He'd shaken off the attack from their father when he'd witnessed his father's lecherous hold on her. He jumped onto their dad's back putting his arm around his throat with as tight of a hold that his young body could muster.

She could see the determination in her brother's eyes. He had always protected her from anything that would bring her harm. Unfortunately, most of the time it was their father. And at the moment their father pried her brother's arms off from around his neck and that's when the battle began. All she remembered was fist flying. There dad throws her brother all around the house. They finally ended up in the kitchen. Her brother got his hand on one of their mothers cast iron skillets and without thought hit their father in the head as hard as he could. And the older gentleman hit the kitchen floor.

Angel remembered there being so much blood. Both she and her brother panicked. They hurriedly grabbed all they could pack into two luggage bags. Her brother had to remind her to become about the body that laid in their kitchen seemingly lifeless. He rushed her towards the front door then stopped and doubled back to the father's body. He carefully rifled through his pockets and retrieved the car keys and his wallet. They made their way to their dad's car. Her brother left the only home she had only known. It was the worst day her life. She seemed to have witnessed her brother kill her dad. It was so horrible. Even if he deserved it.

One minute they we stratigenticly planning a getaway, the next they were running from a scene of a crime. How were they going to get away with this? What were they going to do. Where were they going. She cried so hard she couldn't even recognize the road they had found themselves on. She cried to herself to sleep. When her brother woke her up they were at a motel right in the town where he'd be attending college. He wasn't due for two days, so his plan was to use their dad's credit card to secure a room for two weeks. That way she can just lay low while they continued with their plans.

He had emptied out their dad's bank account which to their great fortune turned out to be a substantial amount. It was easy due to the fact her brother was named after their dad. So, he was able to secure storage for the car until he could get rid of it as well as secure a place for them to stay for. And for A very long time. Her brother figured that it would be at least a few weeks before their dad's body would be found. And even then it just looked like a robbery gone bad. To her it all sounded too neat and too good to be true but clearly God had his hand on them. And her brother was able to attend college, and she eventually got a waitress job to help support herself.

One of the members of her youth group yelled her name bringing her back to the present. She took a huge breath and re-entered the hall where the young group seemed be enjoying ice cream and conversation. And for the most part forgetting about their group leader. Empty paper bowls and plastic spoons were gathered onto a rolling cart. "Sis Angel, I tried to get these hooligans to save you some ice cream. Especially, because I know it's your favorite, but they didn't even listen to me". Her sweet Tim called himself tattling on the older youngsters, which she was suspicious that there's some bullying that will need you be addressed. But at the same time, and weirdly so, that brought a genuine smile on her face.

It just reminded her that this group of eager youngsters were so innocent. They all had a special place in her heart. Thinking how her teenager years were worlds apart from theirs made her suddenly feel responsible for each and every one of them. She just wanted to protect them from the evil that this world has to offer. That evil was always lurking and waiting to devour these precious little souls. She straightened her stance and pressed the imaginary wrinkles out of her perfect Sunday suit and said to herself "NOT ON MY WATCH!".

Chapter 18: Fear and Uncertainty

Just as Trip unlocked his car, gun in hand, determined, focused, angry, bitter...broken, a familiar vehicle pulled directly beside. Almost blocking his ability to open his driver door. He looked directly into the driver's angry eyes, returning his own hostile glare!

His sudden and unwanted neighbor rolled down their passenger window. And after a a few seconds Tripp rolled down his driver's side window down to be met Zipp's angry glare.

"Tripp, man, have you lost your ever-loving mind!! Zipp surprised himself when she noticed his language. EVER-LOVING!! WHAT DOES THAT EVEN MEAN? Then looking around and realizing where he and Tripp where parked, right outside of the city's most popular church's, he figured it had to be in the atmosphere. Because "ever-loving mind, was NOT what he had in mind to say to Tripp.

"What are you doing driving? Especially without your security!! What on earth is going on with you man? You got a death wash or something? If that's what you're about I can ablige, bro. At least with me it'll be quick and painless!! He looked at the church and continued. "I assume you dropped those kids off here, but you've got people for these types of things, man!! What's up?" Zipp continued to blast Tripp all at the same time surveying the area which came second nature. He'd been looking out for Tripp even before Tripp was his name. Heck, even before he'd earned the name Zipp. When Tripp lost his mom, those years ago, Tripp was wild'en out!! Fighting any and everybody that crossed his path!! He was simple an angry young man. They both had attended the same middle school.

They weren't "friends" per say. They weren't enemies either. They just didn't run around in the same circles. Zipp only even came to school because that was where the majority of his clientele was. And he chuckled to himself when he thought that it wasn't even the students that he provided... umm his "pharmaceutical services" too. Of course, there were the usual delinquents who required his services. Which was fine by him. He was an equal opportunity businessman (at the age of 13). But His home life pretty much propelled him to seek employment. And since very few businesses were hiring 13-year-olds, he did what he had to do to help his mom and dad pay bills.

Going without food was bad enough but no gas or electricity AND no transportation was just too much. His parents had provided him and his twin brother with a very good life until the corporation his dad worked for suddenly was shut down due to embezzlement from someone in the higher ranks. Billions of dollars were stolen not from the company but the retirement from every employee that worked for it. He heard about how families were utterly destroyed.

So many committed suicides, leaving there family to add death to their already desperate situation. He was too young to remember all of the details. He could only remember the satisfaction he felt when his parents' eyes lit up when a "secret benefactor" suddenly, out of nowhere 'adopted his family. And the utilities were getting paid. The food was plenty. His parents never ever found out where the blessing came from. They just said that God provided. That once again put a chuckle in his throat. Never thinking of himself as one with all power, even though it was his business that provided the actual funds for his family. Being here outside of a church reminded him of the time he would cry and pray because he found himself forced into a lifestyle, he was absolutely unfamiliar.

But necessity encouraged him to become a fast learner. He had dodged so many near death situations he felt like he was bulletproof. Eventually He came to fear no one. Meanwhile there was this classmate that was known to be squeaky clean that suddenly became the "Mike Tyson" of the school, caught his attention. It wasn't until the two became to blows about some girl that was rumored to be his stepsister, no actually it was his half-sister that Trip found himself involved with. He was young and lost in the game. She wasn't the only female he spent time with.

But, to him, there was something that continued to draw him to her, they continued to spent time together for years in fact. There were times that she'd cut him off and they'd not see each other for months. Probably up to a year. It happened just about three or four times. Eventually she cut off all communication from him. It's been about eight or nine years. Something like that. And fir Tripp, even though this particular young lady just supposedly was his so called "sister" Tripp wasn't having Zipp mess over her. Tripp or rather Trever, which is Tripp's government name, had some weird loyalty to the young chick and he wasn't about to allow him to add her to his small Herum.

So, they found themselves in a fight. Zipp knew he wasn't no slouch when it came to throwing down but was surprised when he found himself clearly over his head when he came up against Tripp. And the fact that Zipp didn't just put a bullet in Tripp, led him to know there was something more to become from their meeting of muscle. He respected the fact that Tripp was not even remotely intimidated by his reputation or his obvious illegal activity. And the fact that Tripp had skills with their hands peaked something else in Zipp regarding their meeting.

He decided to put a little something in Tripp's head about a business plan he'd been wanting to start but needed a business partner that he trusted. This plan would secure their future as well as their families' future and he can finally move on from the street life he was forced to live at his young age. He was already good at what he did. But he was never comfortable. He met with Tripp and explained his plan and to his surprise Tripp didn't even bat an eye. Even the dangerous aspect of the plans. Tripp was a real quick study too and eventually the teacher became the student and instead of Tripp being his guy, he, for lack of a better word, became Tripp's right-hand man.

Quiet as it's kept, they were more like partners, but technically Tripp is the MAN. Tripp rose in ranks in the streets in record time. His respect was legendary in not only in their city, but their state, actually, anyone in the game knew not to even think about crossing Tripp. Or anyone associated with him or his crew. And because they both had great entrepreneurial minds, they went from street business to owning real successful businesses. Which included a chain of clothing boutiques across the country and a fitness/boxing club in four of the country's most popular cities.

Slowly but surely, they have moved from the streets, but the fact that they had to step on a few necks and bust a few heads in the process, they made enemies along the way. Hence the need for heavy security. They've been thru every trauma or tragedy that anyone could ever deal with. Loss of family. Heartbreak. Betrayal. Death threats...most of it was because of bad choices and desperation but a few things were just life. Which made them both lack of trust for anyone. And they both were raised as believers, but life just steered them to only put their trust between the two of them. They had major respect from every member in their crew and they respected their crew.

They actually were like family. But for Tripp and Zipp their bond was iron clad. He finished his angry rant.

"Don't move!!" Zipp backed his car and parked behind Tripp. It was a tight squeeze, but the crowded parking lot didn't give him any other options. He angrily yanked his door open then slammed it and made his way to Tripp's driver side door in what seemed like three steps.

"Man, jump to the passenger side, dude." He said he was still angry as he opened the car door. He immediately saw Tripp's gun in his hand. He pulled out his piece looking around for what he assumed was someone who was coming for them. Tripp immediately told him threw gritted teeth to lower his weapon. He quickly moved to the passenger side of the SUV and motioned him into the driver's seat of his truck. Zipp didn't put his gun away but quickly jumped onto the driver's side of the vehicle still surveying the area. He was still cautious because of the gun he saw in Tripp's hand. He slammed the door then turned towards Trip as he started the car.

"Seriously Tripp. You are TRIPPING!!." He motioned to put the SUV in motion. Tripp quickly reached out and snatched the keys out of the ignition.

"REALLY, BRUH!", Zipp growled at Tripp. "Man, tell me what's going on. What's up? You got your piece out. You are out here without any back-up! Who are you beefing with? Why didn't you call me?!!" Zipp hadn't felt this myriads of emotions in, what seemed his life. He can't believe Tripp would put himself in so much danger. Which would eventually put him and the rest of their crew in danger.

"I'm going to ask again. Man, have you lost your mind?!" He wanted to rake Tripp over, but something kept his language in check. Kept his anger in check. He put away his weapon as he calmed down. He took a large, ragged breath and stared at

Tripp. "Tripp... since that night at the club you've been literally not yourself. Like you're an alien. You experiencing some out of body crap you're not telling me about? What's up!?"

Tripp returned his revolver to his HOLSTER as he put his hand up, halting Zipp's line of questions. "Listen, I already know that you're mad, but I don't have time for your lectures man, there's something that suddenly came up that I've got to take off." He held up his hand again, halting the string of more questions that he knew was right on the tip of Zipp's tongue.

"This is not negotiable, bruh, I have something I have to do right now, so you gotta go man. I'm serious."

Zipp looked at Tripp like he just grew another eyeball...

"Man, I'm not going anywhere." Zip pulled out his gun again and cooked.

"Who we 'bout to smoke?"

"No. Zipp," I said NO! This is personal. It's the last minute. I'm in no danger. And I need you to get back to the house. To make sure things are good. As a matter check on the businesses in the Eastern region. I understand there has been a downward trend with profit. Check on that. I'll look at you when I get back. Zipp just stared at him, laughed. They stopped abruptly. He put his hand on the door handle and motion for Tripp to join him.

"Let do this... whatever we're doing, dude. This ain't even safe. Let's go now, man so we can go!! Now who gettin' smoked?" He opened the driver's side door expecting to see Tripp follow suit. When Trip didn't follow his lead, he closed his door. And glared at Tripp.

"What?!"

"Zipp. Go back to the spot. I'm not playing. I need you to leave now! And that's not a request."

Zipp saw how serious he was, but Tripp needed to understand that he was just as serious and he wasn't going anywhere. The look on his face let Tripp know that he wasn't going anywhere except to handle whatever this business that clearly needed to be handled.

Tripp stood down. He took a breath. He didn't have time to explain the situation, so he gave to shorter version.

He pointed to the small group that were gathered at the entrance of the church.

"You see that older guy he's responsible of the death of my mother and I'm going to kill him."

Zipped turned his head toward the small group at the church's entrance. The whole time he hadn't even noticed that anyone was outside of the church. He'd looked around, he did see anyone... then his eyes zeroed on the you lady. She seemed to be distraught or sick or... his mouth dropped... ANGEL...?

Chapter 19: Truth Revealed

Deacon balanced the pitcher of cold water and crystal glasses, which the church always used for special guests, as he knocked on the closed door of the pastor's office.. He didn't want to disturb the pastor and his guest. He knew traditionally there was always a time of Prayer and preparation for service every Sunday. He just wanted to provide them with liquid refreshments before, what he knew, was going to be a long service. Even tho the visiting pastor resided of a small congregation., He was well known for his humble spirit and his powerful testimony and his ability to inspire all who heard his message. Deacon Douglas had never had a chance to hear the gentleman, however, he couldn't wait. Today was going to be one for the books.

He heard someone ask him to "come in" from behind the pastor's door. So, he slowly entered the room and immediately felt a powerful spirit in the room. The presence was do potent, he almost dropped his tray just in awe of it. He hesitated so he could steady himself. Then moved towards the men of the cloth who were evidently finishing prayer and where, themselves, basking in the presence of peace.

He was both regretful and grateful for his interruption. He had so much respect for his pastor and never wanted to treat the calling frivolously. "If you would please excuse the interruption. I just wanted to offer some refreshing liquids before the explosive day. I know that's the day we are going to have." Then Deacon Douglas apologized again as he prepare to exit the room.

Both of the clergyman rushed in with apologies themselves assuring Deacon Douglas that he was more than welcome and how much they appreciated his service. The three spoke briefly to Threw a few jokes. Then Deacon Douglas looked at his watch, noticing the time.

"I'm mean no disrespect again, gentleman, it looks like time is moving along. Service will be starting in less than ten minutes and I need to check on the rest of our guests Deacons as well as make sure things are in order. The yearly Jubilee was always epic and there were always the little details that needed to be tended to. With everything else. He then poured his pastor and the guest pastor a tall glad of water.

They usually provided the usual bottled water for the congregation but for special occasions they broke out the "good" stuff. Culligan!! He chuckled to himself. He finished his duties and bowed as he headed towards the door. His pastor stopped him before he reached the door handle.

"Hey Deacon, could you do me a favor?"

"Sure Pastor, anything, what can I do for you."

"Could you speak to the youth group leader. I'd like to have everyone in service. I think everyone will receive something special from today's gathering. I can feel it!!"

Deacon Douglas nodded his understanding and silently closed the door on his way out.

The Pastor's excitement about today was a little contagious. It's always a treat to see the young members involved in service. If the Pastor felt it, then it was a guarantee. He hurriedly made his way downstairs to the main fellowship hall where the youth group gathered. Hey, walked in just in time to

see them finishing, of what looked like a snack break by the evidence of the empty Ice cream buckets and plastic spoons and bowls. The volume clearly was the tell-tale of the rush of sugar he was certain everyone was experiencing. He looked at Angel with a 'You poor thing" look on his face. She shrugged her shoulders to let him know this is what she enjoyed about the youngsters. And she wouldn't have it any other way.

"HI Deacon. I'm sorry about the noise. We just decided to celebrate life. And the sugar is contributing to the volume. But look at these faces," They both looked around, saw the whole group engaging with one another. Smiling, and joking. Everyone was participating in the whole youth service. No one was left out. Even the usual shy ones seemed to come to life.

He smiled a big smile. He knew asking her to cover for today's youth group was a great idea. He is now thinking about talking to the board about making this decision permanent.

"If you popped in to tell us to lower it down, I could only say good luck." She shrugged again and laughed in surrender to the madness.

"Actually, I came down because the Pastor wanted to invite the group to joy us in today's special service. The visiting church's youth group will be in attendance, and I know it gonna get lit!"

The whole room went dead with silence at Deacon Douglas' attempt to be cool. Then the laughter that erupted had to have broken the sound barrier and the Deacon couldn't help but join in on the jokes.

He continued to laugh as he turned and headed back upstairs. He waved to everyone in the room as he reminded them to finish up as soon as possible and head upstairs before their guest speaker was in position. That's when Angel sobered up. She suddenly remembered the name that had haunted her just only a little while ago. When the Deacon first said the name, she was shook. She decided that group would just stay downstairs and when service was over, she and her children would make their exit from the the downstairs entrance. She had no evidence that the guy was the guy she thought he was. According to memory THAT guy was dead. It's been years. There's never even been word from anyone about the whole incident. And now she has a family. She knew that she had been covered and protected considering what was done that fateful night. She knew she had been kept from hurt,

harm, danger AND jail. Suddenly it dawned on her... maybe it was because he wasn't dead... what if he was here... using this visit to find her... to destroy her. She could only think of her children. If this really was the Wilmar D. Lawrence Sr, she thought it was, there was only one solution... she'd have taken situations into her own hands. She'd have to kill him, and this time make sure he was dead and he stayed dead.

She clapped her hands getting everyone's attention. It took a few minutes, but the youngsters quieted themselves and gave her their full attention. "OK guys. We have a treat. We've cordially been invited to be a part of today's upstairs service festivities. This was met with boos and sighs and a few "aww man's'... Lonnie was the one to speak up first.

"Why do we hang out with the old folks. We were having tons of fun down here already. Do we have to go?" Everyone chimed in, in agreement. Angel clapped her hands again to quiet the young protectors.

"I understand your concerns guys, but this was requested by the Pastor and if I know anything about mu youth group you are nothing if you're respectful. It's only for an hour or maybe a little over. Their youth group with be in attendance as well. This is a chance to make new friends with a neighboring church and that can open up so many opportunities to do a ton of things outside of just here in our building..." she paused and saw their faces... it seemed as though they were allow the group to continue at upstairs. She continued to display the plastic smile she fixed on her face as she was panicking on the inside. How was she going to grab her kids and make their exit without raising questions from the curious young eyes. That followed her every where she went. She started feeling an anxiety attest coming on. She quickly took some big breaths. She had been running, mentally, it seemed like her whose life.

She was exhausted. She decided that the running would stop today. If she had to end this guy today, then so be it. She was not going to drag any of this group, especially her own children, into her father's evil, toxic world. Yeah, it stops today. She thought as she gathered then guided the young group quietly upstairs to the jubilee. From the sound of music, the guess Pastor was on the Mike and was singing a song, so she reminded the kids to remain quiet and to they take their sears in their designated seats. As they entered the sanctuary, she used her program to shield her face in hopes of not being seen by the visiting pastor.

She wanted to get a look at him first. She didn't have any exact plans as of yet. She'll have to cross that bridge when she gets to it. She made sure that her three children stayed close. Then little Ron tripped making a loud noise causing several members of the church to look their way... including HIM!... she looked up just in time to look into those familiar eyes... All of a sudden, she was her young self. Scared. Nervous. Sad. Bitter... she felt her insides rising up through her throat and she sprinted towards the front entrance where she bumped into someone.. When she looked up, she couldn't believe her eyes.... Darrell!! Her brother?! What on earth.

What's really happening. She looked at a pregnant woman holding his hand as he caught the woman, preventing, clearly the mother of his child, from falling. Darrell., here with a family.?. She noticed that he was wearing the visiting Deacon uniform. She couldn't hold in the inner turmoil any longer as she exploded all over the church front entrance floor. She heard Darrell instructing the woman that was with him to go in and find a seat. He instructed a nearby Deacon to grab a bucket of soap and water and a mop.

And then the door opened up wider to reveal... HIM! She saw her father walking through the entrance, she turned toward the parking lot in hopes of finding sanctuary, somewhere safe. Maybe in her car. Before she had a chance to escape, her dad called her name. His voice still had the authoritive pull that she couldn't run from even in her adult life. "Angel" he repeated her name. Then he recognized his son Darrell was also present. He stumbled back as if he was pushed, and his eyes began to water. "Darrell...Angel... my beautiful children." By this time the congregation had gathered around the entrance of the church and were looking from Pastor Lawrence to Angel to Darrell in both curiosity and confusion.

Pastor Lawrence just fell to his knees at the consternation of everyone. He clapped his hands and gave thanks. Then, he looked at his two children. Well, they were no longer children. He was now crying. Darrell continued to look at him with contempt as Angel was still frozen with fear. "My sweet children. I can't believe you are here!!"

Chapter 20: The Aftermath

Darrell and Chanell arrived at the church late. The last event turned out to be an evening of revelation, truth an healing. They talk well into the night. He had an opportunity to just lay it all bare before his wife and God. He shared with her about how he had to spend the majority of his teen years fighting his father. Especially when he felt a need to protect his sister. It was a hard conversation, but he told her that he had killed his father and it was totally in self-defense. He shared with her how every day he had lived in fear, dreading the inevitable, fateful knock on the door by the authorities because he and his sister were wanted for the murder of their dad. And then there was the identity theft and robbery.

He shared with her all of the things he and his sister had to do to be free of the house of horror that they'd lived in since the disappearance of their mother. And at that moment, the memory of not seeing his mother ever again just released so many emotions. Emotions that he'd kept buried so deep took this to actual feel safe to re-live the whole ordeal and heal from it. He thought to himself... if it hadn't been for that call the other day...

Darell and his wife had just reached the church entrance as someone was coming out, practically knocking them over. And to his surprise it was his sister Angel. Before he could even say her name, he saw HIM... THE DEVIL!! His father! He stepped back and looked up in search of the address. Because, he had to hell or at least a huge mistake. Maybe he was still asleep and was having a nightmare! He looked at his wife and saw the confused look on her face whilst rubbing her midsection checking on their baby.

Chanels' darted from Darrell to Angel than the landed on an elderly gentleman who oddly reminded her of her husband. Same build. Same height. And despite his age the gentleman had the same beautiful curly beautiful hair as her husband. Darrel turned to her and asked her to go into the church and find somewhere safe to sit and he'd be right there in a few minutes. Chanel looked around again and sensed the hostile atmosphere and decided that she wasn't going anywhere until someone let her know what was going on.

Darell spoke in disbelief. He didn't want to believe his eyes.

Angel?!... you and Dad...?!! What's going on? Angel started shaking her head frantically. "No, no, uhm- uhm, no, NO! I don't know where he came from!! She spoke through gritted teeth. Her stomach beginning to turn again. "Then how did he get here?" He was very suspicious of the scene before him.

Then his father spoke. 'I'm preaching here today, son.

Then like they were about to have a wonderful reunion the gentleman exclaimed will joy abd by clapping his hands together as if in prayer. He looked up to the sky, giving thanks to God. Then he looked back at his confused children.

Understandably so. How did they know he was here; was the thought ran through his mind and that was the undoing of him. He bowed his head to the ground and cried even louder, feeling even more grateful.

"My beautiful children. My son, my daughter!! I know this meeting is a surprise. But I believe it was just God!! He's giving me another chance. He is giving me a chance to plead for your forgiveness. I am so sorry. I would even understand if you won't or simply can't forgive me. My behavior to you, my amazing children, was absolutely inexcusable. I was just a broken man who didn't understated about grace and forgiveness.

I never experienced anything like that when I was growing up. And the minute I felt betrayed by your mom, which I eventually found out, the things I had accused her of were not even true, I just fell completely apart. The day I attacked you both I was drunk and heartbroken about your mom."

He turned and faced Darrell. "Son, I don't blame you for having to protect yourselves from me. I was literally possessed. I can't even imagine feeling the way I was feeling and saying the things I said or doing any of the things I did to you both... you are my children. My pride and joy. My family was always my pride and joy. I found out that your mom had been raped as a teenager, and she bore a child from it.

And the house she'd visited was that of her son which was being raised by his grandfather. I thought she was unfaithful. She wanted to tell me but when my heart turned dark, she was afraid. The day I attacked her was the day she was going to introduce us to him...your half-brother. His name is Trevor. The guilt and shame I feel... I can't even describe.

"You killed our mother!!" Darrell spoke through angry tears!!

"No! No, son, I didn't. It may have seemed that way. I was not myself!! Please believe me when I tell you, I don't even recognize that person. Do you remember our life before, I was a completely different individual. Because... I was. I could share with you the horrors I experienced as a child but that'll just sound like excuses. Anyway, when I woke up from that hit on the head, it had been about three days. I was disoriented. There was dried blood from a gash on the back of my head. At first, I didn't know what happened to me, then slowly I began to remember. I was a little dizzy, but I wanted to find you to see if you were safe. I was out of my mind with worry.

I prayed that I hadn't hurt you. I know I was insane. I know... when it was clear that you guys escaped. I reached in my pocket for my keys. I knew I was going to need medical attention. And as you know my keys were gone. So was my wallet. I knew where they were. I prayed that you guys were safe. I called 911. They got me to the hospital and while in the hospital I had a chance to seek to counseling and I continued the therapy for years. It really allowed me to work out so many things from my past that I'd kept buried. Things that were sooner or later going to find their way to the surface. I did track down both of you. Not for any reason other than to give you both my heartfelt apology.

But your lives seemed to being doing just fine and I didn't want to interfere. And as far as your mom goes, I dropped her off in front of a hospital. There were things that happened in her life, on top of the trauma I brought, she needed healing from. After tending to her physical scars, she was also able to receive therapy from a program that helped battered women regain control of their lives. And for her protection she was able to relocate to a different part of the country-protection from me.

When I answered the call in the ministry, I traveled a lot. And ironically ran into her in a Walmart that was located in a small town in Louisiana. She didn't see me. I didn't bother to reach out, well not at that time.

To make a long story and process short, we eventually reconnected. I shared with her everything we knew about you all's lives. Her heart broke every time we spoke. At the same time, she wanted to hear about every detail of your lives. Especially about the grandchildren, she realizes that she hadn't had the chance to love on and spoil them. Even though, clearly the marriage is over, we have a mutual respect for one another that I didn't think I'd ever have. We both wanted to contact you guys and that still is the plan but we just wanted the time to be right... I didn't know this was the both of you guys' place of worship. But I'm glad you're here. Our God's place of worship. But I'm glad you're here. Our God's timing is always different than our timing but perfect, nonetheless.

Darrell spoke up. "Correction, I don't attend either one of the churches. I was asked to help thru the city's local Deacon BOARD ASSOCIATION. Just because the annual "Jubilee" has a reputation of being and epic spiritual experience. So, me and two of my Deacons were just here to help be of service. I really am confused. You're a pastor?"

"Yea, that was my question?" Angel joined in, just as surprised and confused. "When did this happen?" Then the Angel felt more regurgitation.

Their father chuckled in understanding. "Yes. I know I've just dumped a lot for you both to take in. Yes, I am. Our Heavenly Father uses the broken to help heal a broken world. And I was past broken. I was what most people would consider shattered. But God gathered all of my broken pieces, reshaped me and put me back together. A whole new creature. A new me. A healed me. ... a better me. He didn't expect them to believe him. He knew that they would have to see for themselves. Angel back up against the wall next to the entrance door. This is way too much to take in.

Her brother? Her father?!! It had been so long since she spoken to them let along seen them face to face. The only bright part of the whole ordeal is knowing that her mother was alive. And her dad is a preacher. No, not only a preacher but a pastor!! She looked at Darrell and could see he was thinking the same thing. They both said that because they were believers they were supposed to forgive. And people can change. Darrell thought of how in just one day he has become a new man. And Angel had put her permissions life behind her. And was a committed mother and part of a thriving youth ministry. As a matter of fact, she knew that she had changed even more since this morning...since ... since...the call...

Chapter 21: Recovery

"I'm not a Bible thumper or anything like that but killing a preacher has got to be up there on the top three with the "things to do to guarantee bad luck" list, bruh. What could these church folk have possibly done that got you putting a hit on them. You told me your mom left you or abandoned you, some crap like that, when you were a kid. Ain't she the one we need to pay a visit to?" Zipp never had a problem with handling business. That's what he do. But killing Church people made him question Tripp's sanity. Surely there's someone that needed their legs broke for not doing what they're supposed to do or someone who owes them money or anything they could be doing besides bringing bad luck their way?! This just didn't set well with him.

"Man, I done told you, this has nothing to do with you!! Why don't you head back to the crib, make sure we're straight there. Check the books. Make sure we good there. This, right here, is a situation that's long overdue. You can't talk me down or talk to me about it or reason with me because you weren't there and you won't, no, CAN'T understand. It's not a coincidence that all of the people that ruined my life are lined up like sitting ducks. Nah, this has to be handled today. Right now."

Tripp opened the passenger door. The determination on his face convinced Zipp that there was no turning off or turning back. So, he strapped up, jumped out of the car from the driver's side. He didn't care what Tripp said. When there's beef, no matter who it was with, he's always down. This has been the way they have done it since they when the first started. They never knew they'd be in it as deep as they are. They started out just two little knuckle heads trying to make sense out of their situation. His boy needed him. That's all he needed to know.

Both he and Tripp cocked their weapon and headed in the direction of small crowd gathered around the entrance of the church. Tripp was still determined, Zipp was still confused but both men were committed.

As they got closer, Tripp noticed that the crowd had grown tremendously. It seemed as though there was an incident or issue with the members. He saw that there were a lot of teenagers mixed in with the group. That slowed him down tremendously. His issue was simply with just the old man talking to that woman and that dude... he came to a complete stop when he noticed the protruding belly of the woman whose hand the guy was holding.

Zipp stopped when he saw Tripp make a sudden stop, almost plowing into him. He looked towards the direction of their target and saw way more people that had joined the crowd than was there just a few minutes ago. He squinted into his eyes when he notice someone from his past. A woman. It was the only woman that he had ever came close to having a relationship with! Well, it looked like it was her. She, of course, was older. She seemed to be a little more... um fancy... refined maybe...? She was talking to the guy standing with the pregnant woman.

Yea, that had to be her. The drama followed her wherever she went. He decided to get a closer view because if it was here he can finally find out what happened. Why did she start tripping. As he git to bottom of the stairs that led to the church entrance, he noticed a young man helping the young woman. That stopped him in his tracks!!! It was literally like looking at a picture of himself when he was younger... then there was an even younger version of him standing beside the teenage version of him.... He knew they had to be his!!! It all made sense. The times she'd just cut him off without so much a reason. And her preoccupied behavior the last few years there were together. If his memory served him correctly, she disappeared three times. His eyes search for a third young man that looked like him. He didn't find a boy but the young lady that drew his attention reminded him of his mom so much she had to be his!! He's a father?!!

How could she keep something like that from him? Three?!! And two of them were boys!! This changed everything. He headed up the stairs by twos. His hostile demeanor caused everyone who was gathered at the front of the church to look at both he and Tripp. Angel recognized Zipp immediately. She looked at her oldest son with fear. Which made him follow the path of her vision. And looking at an older version of himself caused him to gasp which put both men in defense mode and out of habit the two drew their weapons and pointed at the crowd. This caused everyone to scatter and scream all at the same time. And then. POW!!!

Someone's gun went off!!

Zipp's eyes widened when he realized that he had accidentally discharged his weapon. He saw the three children rush over to the woman that he was certain was his Angelica from years ago. Realizing what he had done, he re-holsters his weapon and closed the gap between the victim in just three steps by taking the stairs by three's.

When got to the church entrance where the woman was laying still, as blood flowed from the wound Zipp confirmed, YEP! It was her. It was his Angel!! What has he done?!! He wedged himself between the frantic children. It doesn't matter how strong a person considers themselves to be, it only takes the urgent cries of a child to reduce you to a simple, human being. Being this close to the children just confirmed is suspicious. It was his Angel and if these weren't his children someone needed to be a sign saying so!! If the situation weren't so dire, he'd spend all of his time getting acquainted with his beautiful family but from the looks of the growing puddle of blood he needs to get Angel help NOW!!

He pulled out his cell and dialed 911, the operator answered immediately, which he was very grateful. He barked at the information of what the emergency and the location. Once he hung up, he pointed to the older young man and asked him to gather as many clean towels as possible from the church that he could. He was about to solicit help from Trip but when he looked around, he was nowhere to be found. As a matter of fact, everyone had ran for cover when his weapon went off. The children were there because their mother was injured.

He couldn't believe what had happened. What on earth is happening. And where is Tripp. If it hadn't been for him, this wouldn't have happened. He held his temper in, he knew he had only minutes to help Angel. He'll just deal with Tripp later.

The young man returned with a pile of towels and Tripp immediately applied two on the wound as he heard the emergency vehicle making its way to the scene. He found himself doing something he hadn't done in almost a decade...almost close to two. But he didn't know what else to do...

As the ambulance pulled up, he jotted down the stars to flag them to the exact spot. He knew they had no time to waste. As the EMT personnel rush up to where Angel's pale body laid, Zipp rush right along with them. The children had to be removed off of their mother's body so they could get to be ark to save her. It definitely was any easy feat.

He had to pull all of them away and the older put up the biggest fight. Zipp could only imagine how they were feeling. He didn't know what to do. He didn't know what to say to these children... his children... which were out of their mind with hurt and uncertainty. So, he just used all of his strength and circled them with his arms and comforted them with positive words. He told them he'll stay right here. And they were safe. They were crying so hard. And he was the one who caused them this inexplicable pain... He held them so close and so tight he was afraid he'd break them, but he couldn't let them go even if he tried. He looked at his newly discovered family.

And he vowed that once this is over, and in his heart, he knew they were going to get past this, he'll be exactly what they need as their father. Just saying that to himself just released something deep in him. He couldn't name what was happening, but he knew he was a changed man. Just like that! He had no doubt. He looked at them again... he was at a loss for words... so he just ... bowed his head and began to pray.

After One a minute or so, of the EMT workers cleared their throat in order to get Zipp's attention.

"Um, I don't know who the next of kin is, but we're on our way to the hospital. We've got the patient stable, but we'll need someone to meet us there to fill out the necessary paperwork. You know, insurance, that type of thing. She may need surgery..." that caused the children to lose it more and Zipped eyed the worker with a warning to find a better way to inform him of what was needed. He caught the warning.

"As I said she's stable. We'll see you there, sir".

The worker scurried into the emergency vehicle. Zipp loosened his hold onto the children just slightly so he can speak to them. When the ambulance pulled off, sirens blaring, he knew he was going to have to get them focused on thinking positively. "Hey, hey, hey" he spoke softly.to the scared. He wanted them to trust him. But on top of dealing with worrying about their mom, he didn't want them to be concerned about being stuck with a stranger. "It's going to be just. My name is

Zipp. I'm going to get you guys to the hospital so we can make sure your mom is given the best care."

He ushered the kids to his car. They were still crying but you can see they were more concerned being there for their mother than their own safety... Ken eyed the nice stranger with a suspicious stare. It was as if he knew something. Zipp gave him a reassuring nod. As he unlocked his car doors. Ken spoke with a shaky voice to his siblings. He did know who this guy was, and he appreciated him but he better understand that he's the man of this family. And if this man tried anything, he would die trying to protect them. "It's OK guys. We do need to get to the hospital so let's let him get us there. Come on, get in. It's ok". He eyed Zipp again over Melanie and Lil Ron's head, letting him know he was not the one. He didn't play when it came to the two getting into his car. And if he even thought this was an easy one, he better think again!!!

Chapter 22: Confrontations

Tripp saw that Pastor Wilmar Lawrence guy retreat into the church when Zipp accidentally let off a bullet. He never took his eyes off the guy. He wasn't standing directly around the people when he was telling about all that has happened to he him theses last couple of decades,. So, he didn't hear everything that was said. But he could have sworn that he heard him say that his wife was still alive. And if that was the truth then that means his mother was still alive. He knew this pastor was also the husband of his mother.

He recognized him from the picture his mom showed him the day she said she was going to introduce him to her family,

The family that he didn't know he had... He remembered being nervous meeting the siblings that he didn't know he had.

He was both nervous and exited. But that meeting never came to pass. As a matter of fact, he never heard from her ever again. No note. Nothing. And now he hears that she's still alive? Why didn't she come back? He learned so much about who he was. He found out that his dad had raped his mom and that was how he was conceived. He figured that she probably decided that she couldn't bear to raise the child of the man who raped her. They thought that it was so easy for her to just let him go. He couldn't believe that she would do such a thing. She was an amazing mother.

Loving, giving, funny...fun. She wouldn't just leave him and not say a word to him. No note. NOTHING! So, it had to be the husband. It had to be. But now he's saying that ... she's alive? What about him? Has she asked about him? Why didn't she love him anymore? He felt silly. Why did it matter. He's a grown man. He probably had more many than any of them. He didn't need any of them and he certainly didn't need some slut who didn't want him!

Even though these thoughts were circling around in his mind, he knew that was not how he really felt. That was just anger and rejection making me feel that way.

"I thought that was you" Pastor Lawrence said to Zipp. He was so deep in thought he didn't know that he had an audience witnessing the myriads of emotions he had displayed on his countenance while he was trying to make heads or tails about this whole situation.

"You're that guy" Zipp simply responded Pastor Lawrence smiled. At Zipp's statement. In his mind Zipp just sounded like a little boy who was still devastated by the loss of a parent. He could imagine the bitterness, anger, hurt confusion that comes either loss in a chest life. There's always the transference of anger. And his anger and all of the emotions Zipp had experienced, as a child when he no longer saw his mother, was transferred to him. "Son, I know how you..."Pastor Lawrence chuckled again. "I don't even know your name, your real name not your street name". He asked almost affectionately.

This young man is his wife's child so by proxy he was his child. And he had made the mistake of not doing the right thing when he had a chance or bring the person he was called to be, and he vowed to never make that mistake ever again. "Why.?!" Zipp was angry still. "Why do you need to know?" "Well son, it seems on some level we are connected and I just wanted to know what to call you?" "You can call me Zipp", he replied on the defense. "Ok...OK.... Zipp." He didn't want the young man to feel threatened or defensive. He wanted Zipp understand that even life did its best to make them enemies, they weren't. This broken young man standing before him with clenched fist, needed to know that this world didn't want him to know that he was seen. And all of his mistakes and bad decisions didn't stop him from being considered. He wanted him to know that's he was loved. He wanted Zipp to know that he can find "home" in his relationship with him.

"I'm not the enemy. You don't have to feel threatened by me or those other three that I know you realize are your half siblings. I... have ...made some of the worst decisions. And they have effective so many lives in a negative way. I know I can't take bake the things I've done... I can only express my deepest regret and my most sincere apology."

The Pastor began to walk toward as Zipp slowly. He did want him to think this was nothing more than a chance to heal. To get pass the past a move forward to a better future. He knew what this was a God thing. Suddenly seeing both of his children AND the son of his wife in a matter of minutes had God's name all over it. So, he now went to put it all in God's hands.

He continued to walk to Zipp, both hands slightly raised to prove he posed absolutely no threat. He was finally standing directly in front of Zipp. They were eye to eye. And his expression was one of sincere sorrow and repentance.

"You have every reason to hate me. To be angry. To be even want to kill me. But let me warn you... it's not going to make you feel any better. It'll just feed the monster that has been living within you. That monster was crested to protect your heart. I know, son. Because I had the same demon living within me. And it wasn't until I gave all my anger and bitterness away to someone who was better equipped to deal with it that I became a whole. No longer broken." He relaxed his whole body and put his hands in his pockets.

He spoke to the young boy in him that wanted to no longer fall abandoned.

"Chandler, everything is going to be just fine. You have to know that you were never alone. You have had the best protection that not even money could buy. And son, know that you are loved." He embraces him once again. Vowing to never leave this young man's life ever again.

Chapter 23: Revelation

Zipp and his three passengers arrived pretty much at the same time the ambulance did, which was no surprise considering how fast Zipp had been driving. It was definitely an act of God that he hadn't been pulled over by the police for speeding and reckless driving. He had switched lanes, ran lights broke speeding laws to ensure that he and these children... his children, he was still reeling about that fact, but his he and his children needed to be there to make sure Angel was getting everything thing she needed from the doctors so they can have that conversation that had been postponed way to long. Zipp pulled up in a parking spot marked emergency and instructed the kids to get out of the car to make is quick. They had no time to waste.

He and the kids half walked, half jogged, half sprinted to the emergency entrance. The automated doors opened entirely too slow for Zipp's taste. Zipp was never known for his patience and everything happening today was pushing his patience to the limit.

He hurriedly ushers the youngsters thru the security process and the rushed to the receptionist area enquiring about Angel and her statistics.

"Sir, if I can get you to slow it down. I can really understand you", the lady behind the bulletproof glass partition slowly responded to the urgent behavior Zipp was showing. She worked in the emergency department and was so used to everyone thinking if they yelled at her, rushed her, even threatened her, that their loved one's situation was going to magically resolved or there healing was instant. But, in her field she had seen the most heartbreaking situations and the only thing anyone could do was to calm down.

Looking at the pleading faces, she figured this was his family and the woman in question was his wife and their mother, but she needed to them to just calm down. "Sir, the woman your enquired about, just arrived and hadn't been completely registered, however, here are the forms needed so we can begin to care for whatever her injury is.it gives us permission to do what is needed including surgery if it's required." Zipp grabbed the clipboard full of firms and turned to his little family. He knew they wanted answers right now, but she needed them to do exactly what the young lady asked. "OK, we need to get these filled out as fast as we can. Since you guys know all of Angel's information, I'll fill out the paperwork but I'm going to need you guys to provide all the information so we can get her the proper care so we can get her taken care of.

Ken and Melanie looked at one another when this stranger, that they've never met, said their mother's name. They both had their suspicions especially for Melanie.as she looks from her brother to the stranger. Even a baby could see that they definitely related. How is the question. And Ken was thinking the same thing. He looked from his sister to the stranger and almost gagged when he realized that she looked just like the guy with longer hair and lip gloss… which would have been both gross and hilarious at the same time if circumstances were different. "OK but you're going to have to tell us who you are. Sir, after we get these forms filled out". He had his own conclusions, but he needed to hear it from this guy.

Zipp gave him a look and a nod confirming what he knew the youngblood was thinking as well giving him his word that when the time is right they were going to have a conversation. A conversation that was going to rock as well as change both of their lives. Ok after that was established the went about the business of filling forms. Melanie continued, consoled Lil Ron who had no idea what was going on. All were thinking that he wanted his mom, and he wanted her right now. She was bleeding!!? Why was she bleeding?!!. Why wasn't she here with them right now? Who is this stranger?! He didn't like him. He needed to go away, and his mother needed to come here right now!!

Melanie had to catch his as he began to fall to his needs. Her pour little brother was beside himself with hurt. They all were. She tried to pull him onto her lap, but Lil Ron shook his head, refusing to get off the floor.

"I need to pray for mommy!! I want God to bring her to me now. I know he can make her all better and I'm going to ask him to do it!!"

He was committed to his conversation with God and there was not one thing that anyone could say to stop him or change his mind. So, there was nothing else to do but to join him. So, Ken and Melanie, both joined there little brother on the floor. They both got on their knees and grabbed hands and began to pray.

Zipp was out of his element here. When there was a situation that needed to be dealt with, he just usually was locked and loaded and out the door. He didn't depend on anyone. Not even his boy, Tripp. It had only been him alone that took care of him. That was his understanding. But as he finished putting in the information, he gathered Ken to provide for the hospital. He returned the forms to the desk also informing the receptionist that whatever wasn't covered by her insurance he'd pay for by pocket.

When he returned to the kneeling children, he knew there was nothing left to do but join them. He kneeled down and grabbed Ken's hand. When he looked at his tear-filled eyes at Zipp he tried his best to let his look at him was telling him he and his siblings are all going to be OK. And that he had them. But Ken's look at him let him know that God had this whole ordeal in control. Zip nodded his understanding and his complete surrender of what thought he had, control. He knows he had no control over what happens to Angel. To anything. He now knows he never did.

Zipp began to pray. He didn't really know the correct way to do this. He did know the words to say. He wasn't even sure God would even listen to him. He was so sorry that his hot-headed, -don't trust anyone- don't need anyone attitude towards life has ultimately caused this family, his family ounce of pain. They continued to, in spite of the curious onlookers, pray and cry. And cry and pray while Zipp continued to stay as strong as he could because if the goes the other way he was going to have to really step up. And he would have to step into a life he had absolutely no knowledge of. But something tells me that someone, somewhere, somehow has qualified him.

And he suddenly felt a confidence and strength that would rival Superman.

He bowed his head and joined in prayer with the children. After what seemed an hour, someone tentatively tapped him on the shoulder not wanting to disturb the family's commitment to their faith. Zipp looked up, anticipating good news.... The nurse spoke solemnly to Zipp and the kids. By the look at their face, it didn't look like good news, but he kept his thoughts positive. "Mr. Bryant". Zipp's actual name was Anthony Bryant. He rose from the kneeling position he had been in with the children. They had stayed in prayer the whole time they were waiting for the doctor. The nurse led them to a room where families met to discuss their loved one's condition. And what would be needed to get them back to one hundred percent. They continued to think positive thought. Their mother had to be o.k... It was their mother. They had no one else to take care of them. God wouldn't let anything happen to her.

"The doctor will be with you in a second." The nurse left the room with the same solemn look on their face. It made Zipp a little nervous. But he kept his thoughts positive.

The doctor walked in with the same solemn countenance. And Zipp had to take a big breath. He realized how many families he had put in this exact position. Would these innocent children have to be punished for his bad decisions? He took another big breath which drew Ken's attention. He has to get it together. He had impressionable no eyes paying attention.

"Ok Zipp get it together. You gotta be "Strong. He said to himself. Giving himself a little pep talk. He immediately asked God for forgiveness for the things he done. It never occurred ti him the carnage of he and his crew's behavior. That it was someone child, brother, mother, sister... that everyone was someone to someone. He couldn't even count how many families he had put in thus position. And the irony is that it was he who put his own family in this very predicament.

He looked at the doctor and at this point expecting the worse. That's what he deserved. He looked at the kids. But they didn't.

Chapter 24: New Beginnings

Tripp suddenly pulled away from the Pastor. He didn't know how he was supposed to feel. He didn't allow himself to feel. That way you'll never be hurt. He had allowed anger and bitterness to fuel his whole reason to live. To do everything in his power to not have to need anyone. To always be the boss. Always be on top and land on his feet. To be the one to be feared and respected. He suddenly remembered something his mother had instilled in him, this was before she abandoned him, he thought angrily. She always instilled in him to be a kind person to everyone and to forgive every time. And to remember that you don't know what people have gone or ARE going thru. He just froze. He just wanted to... kill someone...

something!! He turned around facing the pastor, drawing his weapon and pointed it at him.

"You are not going to get away from taking my mother away from me. I was only a little boy, man!! My grandfather was the worst person to leave me with to raise me. He didn't care about anything and clearly, he didn't know a thing about caring or raising anyone. Look what kind of man his son turned out to be. Somebody needs to die!!!"

The Pastor did seem to be moved, scared or anything. He just put out his hand and spoke. "You are so correct son. And believe it or not someone did die. But there is so much I would love to share with you about that."

Tripp's eyes git bug, "You told your kids that she wasn't dead!! He was just about to pull the trigger. When the Pastor said quickly, "She isn't. "I wasn't talking about your mother, son.... Give me the weapon. I promise you I'm here for you. I'll never abandon you, so..."

He kept his hand extended until Trip slowly, with hesitation, handed over the weapon to the pastor. Then the phrase "I'll never abandon you" was his undoing. That was the worst feeling. To not feel worthy for someone to stick around. He didn't even have any memory of his dad. He had nothing to even reference. As a man without a man to teach him about being a man allows you to just use your imagination. T.V....

books. But for him to actually hear those words spoken to him...

Pastor Lawrence carefully took the weapon. It came to mind the things that he probably used with the offensive object for. And knowing that he inadvertently had an influence in the direction that this young man took and it just confirmed to him that this young man still needed someone positive in his corner.

There were probably a lot of things that was missed in his life. He silently paid for strength and direction. He had many things that he needed to make up for. His children. His grandchildren. His wife. He was grateful that she never divorced him. And that led him to believe that there is hope.

There was a knock on the door that startled them both. Tripp turned his back and straightened his face. He couldn't have it out on the streets that he was at church crying.

Someone frantically opened the door.

"I'm sorry to interrupt." It was the hosting pastor.

"I just received a call saying when that weapon went off one of our members was hit!"

"What?!" Both Tripp and the Pastor spoke in unison.

"Who?" Pastor Lawrence had a bad feeling.

"It was Sis Angel". He rushed past the two, to his desk and grabbed is crucifix and his bible. Then they turned and pointedly spoke to the both of them.

"It may be a good idea for you both to come with me. I don't think she's not doing well."

He stood holding the door, waiting for the two men to join him to the ride to the hospital.

All three of the gentlemen didn't waste another second as they headed out. Pastor Lawrence was at his wits end. His daughter!!! No. No. No. Nooo!!!! He just got her back in his life. He needed to make things right. He owed it to them that!! He quickly got himself together. He remembered he was different. He no longer reacted on impulse. All it takes is for one desperation situation to occur and if your faith isn't strong, you'll find yourself back to where you started. And that's a road where he refuses to go back. They seemed to have great success with traffic lights. They were green the whole way and all were thinking the same thing. And the three were grateful. Even Tripp. He hasn't even had a chance to meet his sister, well half-sister. And once again, for just a few minutes, he was a child again. He gave himself a mental and physical shake. Being that he was sitting in the back seat no one saw his struggle.

They arrived at the emergency entrance and quickly jumped out of the car and rushed to the reception area. Unfortunately, there was a line. Both pastor's flashed there clergy so that granted them immediate access to the front of the line. When Tripp began follow them, reluctantly Pastor Lawrence, leaned in.

"Son, it might be a good idea for us to handle this initially. When it's safe we'll send a nurse."

Tripp understood. There are a million things running through his mind. He had been living thus life for a very long time. It's the only life he knows. And he feels lost. Death is something he deals with often, so it doesn't faze him. But the thought of something knows. Well, wants to know had him rethinking everything he knew about himself.

He took a pulled out his phone and called Zipp, thinking to himself how weird that he had been gone and neither Zipp or any of his crew tried to contact him. The line rang three times before Zipp barked a

"What's up".

"Hey bruh, Where are you?"

"Yea, I'm at the hospital. That woman at the church was Angel and she got hit by my bullet. I'm here with kids." Zipp paused and Tripp heard some muffled voices. Zipp returned. "The pastor is here. I gotta go. I'll call you".

The line went dead. So Zipp is here with his. Well, whatever they are to each other. I made him feel a certain way. He also felt that he should be there. So, he went to the receptionist's desk as ask for the room for Angel Lawrence, his sister. He wasn't lying. It was the truth. It didn't matter that they had never had a chance to officially meet. Only thru pictures and stories from his mom. But families are associated from even less facts. The receptionist gave him the room number and let him know that she was just now recovering from surgery and are only allowing visitation from her children and parents access. And that was only for a few minutes. But he can have a seat in the waiting room on the floor where she was recovering. He nodded his thanks a headed toward the elevators. He took a breath. The elevator dinged, signaling that he reached her floor. He followed the directions that lead to the waiting room for patients in recovery. The closer he got to the waiting room he heard the sound of family mingling and laughing as they waited for their loved ones to heal and be released. He walked in the waiting and came face to face with ...his niece and nephews...?

Chapter 25: Last Call

Ken, Melanie and Lil Ron sat quietly in the waiting room. When the pastors walk into their mom's recovery room they were immediately ushered out and led into their current position. The look on all three of their faces showed that they we spent. The day was an emotional roller-coaster. Ron's head was bobbing back and forth. He was past exhausted, but he was not going to go to sleep until he heard his mother's voice, and he got to tell her how much he loved her.

Melanie was still angry about the whole situation. The stranger who drove them was able to stay in the room but her own children have to wait outside for someone to tell them whether she was going to live or... she couldn't even finish the thought as a tear rolled down her cheek.

Ken looked up at some guy that just walked into the waiting room. Their eyes locked, the Ken looked away. The older guy looked like he was about that life and Ken didn't want any trouble. His mind was still on his moms condition. And how his siblings were holding up. At the same time, he'll just keep an eye on the guy...just in case. In case of what he didn't know, but whatever it was, he wasn't going to make it easy.

"That had to be them". Trip thought to himself. And what took him by surprise was...they have got be Zipp's kids.! Man, it was like looking at Zipp at the age they started hanging out. Seeing them almost knocked him over. Yeah, those were his kids. He couldn't deny them if he tried. But when did this all happen. He thought he told him to stay away from his "sister". Back then, he loved that fact that he could take on the role as the protective brother. Even if it was only in his mind. Being an only child and being raised by an old man who could give a rat's backside, had to be some kind of torcher for any child.

And there was the whole disappearing act from his mom, so he was like Mike Tyson ready to beat the breaks out of anybody he deemed needed it. He wasn't a bully. He was what you'd call a "finisher". He never started any fight, but it was his pleasure to finish it. He spoke to himself, yea, he knew he had issues. But his issues kept him from being a victim. And even though he and Zipp had to come to blows from time to time, he has never outright been disrespectful. And secretive. But the proof is sitting right in front of him. Times three.

Zipp needed to have his neck grabbed and his feet dangled. Trip made a mental note to have a little conversation with his homeboy. He is a hardheaded clown. He might have to soften that head a little bit. He pulled out his cell phone to see if he could just find out what was going. The line rang several times before Tripp decided to hang up. Sitting around was not his thing. And knowing that he was literally sitting in a room with ...family. He was a bit anxious, which was a feeling that was completely foreign to him. He stood up and started to pace.

Melanie noticed that the new person that joined them in the waiting room kept looking over to her and her siblings. So, she kept an eye on him. He wasn't giving creeper vibes. He looked like he had something he wanted to say. She looked over to Ken to see if he sees what she sees. And yep, Ken had a bead on him. He eyed the guy with a massage all on his face. Being that he always considers himself the man of the house he took it very seriously. The guy didn't seem to care what message Ken had for him, though. He looked like he wanted to talk to him. Them. The guy also seemed anxious or confused. Then Ken realized that he was the guy who was with the guy who is in the room with his mom...surroundings... AND SO WAS THE GUY THEY RECEIVED A RISE TO THE HOSPITAL!!!

Ken noticed that the guy was coming their way. He jumped up ready for protect his brother and sister.

"Hey there, youngblood." Tripp spoke to Ken. He didn't sound. Threatening. His demeanor was completely layed back. He still seemed anxious. The two men both dapped like there was a secret understanding of how to greet one another. Ken's should relax. He didn't feel he needed to be on the defense. However, what did he want?

Tripp completely saw everything and respect the young man fir handling his business.

"What's up?" Ken's response was short and to the point.

"I'm not one to skirt around an issue. So, I'll go straight to the point"

Ken's shoulders were up again. Trip smirked.

"I think we're here for the same reason. I was at the church. I dropped off some kids that needed a ride and I recognized someone."

Ken was curious. Who could this guy know who went to the church?

"It was the Pastor who was a guest or something. But anyway, we have a weird history. My man that was with me made a serious mistake and a woman got hurt".

"Why are you here?!" Ken was now on complete defense. The guy just reminded him why he and his siblings were here. And if he was here to hurt his mom, he is in for a fight.

Tripp noticed the young man's balled up fists and flared nostrils and he put his hand up.

"Nah, youngblood it's nothing like that. It's really a long and serious story and I don't have a lot of time to tell it. But I do believe before we leave today, you'll find out what I'm talking about."

Ken was about let the guy know that if he wanted a problem, he was ready. But before the two gentlemen could finish, a nurse peeped onto the waiting area and ask if any family was there for Angelica Lawrence.

Ken and his made their way towards the waiting area exit and to their surprise the guy that just spoke with Ken headed towards the exit as well. Ken rushed his siblings to the door not knowing what the man was up to, but he knew that they needed to get to their mom and find out what's was going on. When all four seemed to be heading in the same direction, Ken turned around and blocked the hall.

"What are you doing? What do you want. You better not be here to hurt my family. This is a hospital and there are police all over this place so if I were you, I'd turn around before I get to yelling!!

Trip took a big breath. He was not in the mood to teach a boy, who was probably his nephew, a lesson about threatening a man. It has big the longest few days of his life. He did respect the little fellow. He decided to tell him the truth.

"Little dude, I'm not here for no beef. I just found out that your mom is my aunt, so I think I'm your uncle.

I'm just as shocked as you guys are, and this is not how I wanted to meet you. But that's not important right now. We need to find out how she is doing. And I'm exhausted and I'm not in the mood so let the nurse take us to her"

The three kids were so shocked and confused that no one had anything to say. Tripp's no-nonsense expression propelled them to follow the nurse. They slowly open the door to Angel private room.

Observing the hospital personnel, the pastor's and the guy that gave them a ride to the hospital.

In spite of the urgency of the moment, the children confused expression let the adults in the rooms know that someone needed to start explaining.

Pastor Lawrence felt like he was responsible for the confusion that caused the issues happened today, so he cleared his throat so he can explain it to the young family the best that he could.

"Come in. You are amongst family. Your mom has been waiting to see"

The Pastors and Dr. moved aside to reveal Angel, eyes partly open. Her bed was set on a ninety-five-degree incline. So, she was in a sitting position and in perfect view to see the beautiful faces of her children.

Ron was the first to burst into a short jog. His squeals of happiness encouraged his other two siblings to join in, in the expression of love to the mother.

"Mommy!!" Ron couldn't control the tears of happiness to see his mom. And it seemed that the older siblings had been holding in their tears but in seconds the three were in their mother's arms. Crying and kissing and hugging their mother. Angels' hospital opened again as Darrell and his pregnant wife walked in. He clearly had not expected the crowd that was present in her room. But.it seemed to have an atmosphere of Jubilee and joined in what seemed to be a happy occasion so he guessed that Angel must be out of danger...

He thought introducing himself would help the looks of question on a couple of faces.

"Hl everybody. I'm Darrell Lawrence, well Will Darrell Lawrence, Jr. I'm an Angels brother. And this is my wife, Chanel.

Everyone seemed to be in the spirit of "the more the merrier", so everyone welcomed Darrell and his wife.

Angel's children were still lavishing love on their mother clearly oblivious to the growing number of people in their mother's room. The Doctor didn't ignore and knew that it can be detrimental to Angel's recovery to have this many individuals. She is going to need to get plenty of rest before she is considered out of the wood.

So, the Doctor reluctantly had to remind them all that their Angel just had surgery, so they have got to a little easy on her with the visitation. Just for now. Not wanting to spoil the emotional moment he quickly interjected.

"But by all means let her know that your glad that she is doing well, and has your support. Also, as the attending physician, I can officially say the surgery was a success. She lost so much blood, tho, however and ironically, we had the perfect match in our blood bank, so I'd say today was the win. It was a bit of a miracle considering how rare her blood type is. I believe it was a sibling from the results from the lab. A sibling or a child.

Angels' children were too young to have been the donor. Everyone turned and looked at Darrell.

"I'd like to say it was me, but I've never donated blood." Darrell shrugged his shoulders in confusion. Every looked around the room trying to figure out where their donation came from. Darrell was her only sibling... or is he? Ken remembered what the guy in the waiting room said.

"It was you, wasn't it?" He looked Tripp daring him to deny it.

Tripp had nothing to hide. "That's probably the truth, youngblood". Tripp casually nodding his head. "I donated blood about a decade or so ago when money was low and I needed seed money. Looks like someone, somewhere knew it was going to be needed, so..."

Tripp shrugged his shoulders with a cavalier attitude ignoring the fact that his donating blood those years ago just saved someone's life. Heck! Saved his sister's life!

Zipp wasn't surprised about Tripp. During their whole friendship he always found some way to be the hero. Providing a family with groceries, providing Christmas gifts for families. He would randomly give back to the community. It was anonymous but Zipp was over the books. He always knew. He shook Tripp's hand and gave him a brief pat on his back as the crowd were leaving Angel's hospital room.

Not wanting to leave but knew he had to, Lil Ron broke Melanie's hold on his hand and ran back to give his mom one last hug.

He must have pulled out a wire or unhooked something because suddenly the emergency monitor went off. Everyone was rushed out of the room as hospital staff filled the room.

Lil Ron felt so bad and scared he called out hoping he didn't hurt his mother. No one could calm him down he continued to yell for his mom "Mama!! Mama!!" Lil Ron yelled nonstop. "Mama!! Please, no!! MAMA!!!

The cries from her youngest son shocked Angel back to consciousness. She looked around. "...Ron, baby...

Epilogue

Angel looked around the room. She looked at Ken and Melanie as he looked down at her frantically. And Lil Ron had his head on her chess ass he continued to cry and yell her name. She grabbed Ron by his arms and pulled him away from her. She was so confused. How did she get here. She was laying on the floor at the bottom of the stairs at her house. Her children were crying and her head right foot was killing her.

"Ron baby it's o.k. I'm OK baby. She pulled him close to quiet his cries.

"Mom!! You're awake!! We thought you were... something bad happened to you!" Melanie said between gasp of air while she wipes her tear-stained face.

Angel heard the sound of an ambulance driving on their block then stopped right outside of her house. "Is that for me?" She said, still not understanding the house she got on the floor at the bottom of the stairs AT HER HOUSE?

Ken noticing her confused expression filled her in. "Yea mom, you fell downstairs, remember. You went to get your Bible, and you were on the phone as you rushed down the stairs in tines latter's you call shoes. I told you to stop running down the stairs in those death traps". He opened the door and guided the EMT'S inside of the house and pointed to his mom on the floor with the twisted foot and the knot on the forehead.

"What, WAIT!? How long have I been here on the floor? Was I unconscious?" She seemed disoriented to her children. They just credited to the horrible fall she took on their stairs.

"Yes, mom you fell down the stars. You were out for like ten minutes. You scared us to death!! We didn't know what was going on with you?" Melanie almost sounded like she was mad. Angel didn't understand what was happening. So, she never went to church. Or was in the hospital... or. She did finish her thought because the emergency workers got busy taking her temperature, asking her and her kids questions as to what happened. Everything happened so fast. Before she knew it, she was strapped to a gurney. She yells for the emergency workers to stop!!

"What about my children?" She wasn't just going to just leave them. She still had questions. Ken calmed her down." Don't worry, mom, we called Uncle Trevor right after we called 911. See?" He pointed to her brother's car as it was pulling 70iinto the driveway behind her car. He stopped the EMT'S and asked them where they would be taking her. Before anyone could answer the question, everyone saw Lil Ken running towards Angel holding her cell phone. "Mom, your phones ringing."

Angel grabbed the phone and saw the call log said, "Caller Unknown " she deleted the call and gave it back to her son She looked at her brother, Pastor Darrell Lawrence, "Darrell could you make sure the kids get to the hospital?" "Sure, I got you Babygirl. You know I'm always here. I'm here until the end of time. Angel's eyes widened as she shot straight up on the gurney...